Nobody's Dog

Other Lions titles you may enjoy

Joyce Stranger
Midnight Magic

Caroline Akrill
The Eventing Trilogy
Eventer's Dream
A Hoof in the Door
Ticket to Ride

Patricia Leitch
The Jinny series
1. For Love of a Horse
2. A Devil to Ride
3. The Summer Riders
4. Night of the Red Horse
5. Gallop to the Hills
6. Horse in a Million
7. The Magic Pony
8. Ride Like the Wind
9. Chestnut Gold
10. Jump for the Moon
11. Horse of Fire
12. Running Wild

Animal Sanctuary

①

Nobody's Dog

Joyce Stranger

Lions
An Imprint of HarperCollins*Publishers*

I owe thanks to Ann Cragg and Barbara Emptage of
the Glantraeth Animal Sanctuary, Anglesey,
for letting me share their weekends and "borrow"
their animals for my stories.
To Eileen Clark who rescued the real Blue,
and to Joe Naylor of the Brynterion working farm
for letting me watch a breach calving.
To David, Alison and Mark at the sea zoo
which I have watched grow.
To Les and Denise Edwards whose bitch Jess and
dog Nikos have given me the best pup I ever had.

*The stories in this trilogy are works of fiction; the
events are imaginary; the characters, farms and
villages bear no resemblance to any person or place.*

First published in the U.K. in 1992 in Lions

Lions is an imprint of HarperCollins Children's Books,
a division of HarperCollins Publishers Ltd,
77–85 Fulham Palace Road, Hammersmith,
London W6 8JB

Printed and bound in Great Britain by
HarperCollins Book Manufacturing Ltd, Glasgow

Chapter 1

It was a deep ditch but it was a dry ditch. Martin, all the breath knocked out of him, lay on his back. He stared morosely at a sky streaked with wind whips that flew beneath the sullen clouds. Long trails of grey mist. Mares' tails.

He scrambled to his feet, even more furious than before. The old ewe glared at him. He knew she hated him as much as he hated her. He was quite sure that she had deliberately pushed him into the ditch. He knew she hated him as much as he hated her.

Martin kicked a stone out of the road into the long grass. He was angry and he intended to stay angry. He wanted to shake the ewe and yell at her, but he knew that would only make matters worse. If they could be much worse.

The day had started with the overturned milk bottles on Taid's doorstep. Martin had protested that it was not him, but the rest of the family were convinced it was. They were by now used to his naughty tricks, his deliberate acts to annoy them.

But Martin had not broken the milk bottles, and he thought the ewe had done it. Resentment flared in him. This time, he wasn't to blame, but it didn't make any difference.

He grabbed at the ewe's fleece.

"You bring her back, boy," his stepfather had said, when he'd discovered that Martin had let the ewe out. "And then no more will be said. If you don't . . ."

Martin had no idea what would happen if he failed. He decided it would be better not to find out. They might have very unpleasant ways of punishing you in Wales. He felt as if he were in a foreign country as well as with a strange family. He disliked and distrusted them all. Dilys and Anna Wyn, his stepsisters, who would whisper together in Welsh. He was sure they were talking about him.

He knew he should try and learn the language. Taid, his step-grandfather had even offered to teach him. "Learn it," he'd said, "and then you will be part of us too. We have always spoken Welsh on the farm, Bach, and we forget you don't know it. No harm meant."

Martin had at least learned the word Taid,

which was pronounced Tide, and meant Grand-father. But the rest was meaningless. He didn't want to be a part of them.

Martin's mother was taking Welsh lessons, and that just compounded his hurt. He felt as if she were betraying him all over again. He had been furious with her when she told him she was going to marry the Man, and he'd have two step sisters. He was still furious. Sometimes he was so miserable that he felt sick.

Why had they had to move to this miserable place? Why had she had to marry again? Martin didn't want a new family. He was quite happy living with his mother in their flat outside Chester. But now all that security was gone, taken away and replaced by what? A cold, dank farm and a family he didn't want.

He pushed the thoughts away and tried again to make the ewe walk the way that he was going. She stood with her black woolclad legs locked. Her mean slanting eyes glittered in her black face. He grabbed at the grey wool on her back.

Martin had never lived with animals before. He didn't like them and he didn't intend to like them. They didn't like him either.

The town had been cosy with houses all around. Here there were wide skies and far horizons and the green fields stretched drearily and endlessly, divided by bleak hedges. The wind blew ferociously and it rained. How it rained.

He hauled again at the heavy fleece. The Man had no right to make him fetch her.

Martin refused to give his new family their names, even in his thoughts. Except for Taid. The old man had his respect, and he often stood up for Martin when everyone else was angry with him.

"I hate you, you stupid creature. Why did you have to run away?" he asked the old ewe, even more furious with her for her awkwardness.

Never mind that it was his fault she was out. She didn't have to go through the gate, though he had hoped she would. Hoped she would run off and never be seen again. She had been a pet lamb, long ago, orphaned and bottle reared.

"No use to man or beast," Gwyn said when she had raided the kitchen and stolen the new baked bread, or had spent an afternoon bawling for someone to come and pet her. He laughed as he said it and rubbed her on her woolly head. She butted his arm gently, aware that nobody ever grumbled at her.

Martin wanted the ewe lost because the two Girls doted on her, and were daft about her. Fussed her and petted her and behaved as if she were part of the family. He spent a great deal of time thinking up ways of upsetting them.

The older Girl annoyed him most. She worked as a veterinary nurse at a big practice over on the other side of the island. She was always impatient with people, bad tempered and bossy, but so very gentle with the animals she nursed.

Yesterday she had brought home yet another injured bird. The barn already had cages in which were a bad tempered kestrel that had flown into an electricity line and injured its wings, and a seagull with a broken leg. There was also an injured duck that had tangled with either a cat or a fox.

Martin would not admit to anyone, least of all to himself, that he was afraid of all animals, and terrified of dogs. They were creatures that stared at you, and snarled at you. And bit.

He never had been bitten. No dog had ever snarled at him, but he could read the papers like anyone else. The papers said that dogs were very treacherous and that people ought not to have them.

He reckoned this old ewe was dangerous too. Like any other pet, she had a name. It was Blodwen, but everyone called her Cariad which was crazy because it meant darling, and if any creature wasn't a darling it was Blodwen. Her dirty fleece was shaggy and she stank. She had strange light eyes that seemed to assess Martin and find him lacking in every way. She had long yellow teeth. She had a daft expression when she didn't look enraged, as she did now. She could lift her lips back like a dog.

She was more like a dog than a dog, the older Girl said, proving to Martin that he was quite right in thinking all girls were stupid and these two more so than most.

Martin had been proud, for just a few minutes, of opening the gate and watching the ewe trot determinedly down the road. That would be the end of her.

But the Man, his stepfather, had seen him. He had been coming out of the barn, where the ewes that had just lambed were kept.

His stepfather hadn't been angry. Sometimes Martin wished he would be angry. He wished the Man were cruel so that he could glory in his misery. As it was there were times when he felt silly and he didn't like that at all. Nor would he admit it, even to himself.

He tried to provoke anger because maybe then the Man would want him and his mother to go away. They could go back to their cosy little flat, just the two of them, with his mother talking to no one but him and thinking of no one but him. He sometimes ached with that need.

He tugged at the ewe, and she stamped her front hoof and stood still in the road as if she were made of rock.

"She's old, and she doesn't understand traffic," the Man had said. Gwyn his real name was, but that was another name Martin didn't intend to use, not even in his mind. It would mean acceptance.

His own father hadn't been much of a father. He had left them one fine day when Martin was only five years old and newly at school, and his mother had spent a year crying. They had moved from the big house with the huge garden that had been such fun, into the tiny flat.

His father had come to see him once, and then his mother's letter asking for more money for them both had come back from the post office marked "Gone away. Address unknown."

He knew his father had married again and had a new family of three little girls. He'd gone to Australia. They still saw his father's mother, but even she had no idea where her son now lived.

Granma lived far away, down in Sussex. Martin wondered if he could hitch a lift to Hastings and stay with Gran. She'd understand how stupid it was for his mother to marry again and take on a whole new family.

"Will you come along?" he said to the ewe, his voice furious. He pulled her ear.

Enraged, Cariad glared at him. Then, quite deliberately, she kicked him. Her hard hoof caught him on the shin. He was sure the horrible animal had broken his leg.

He stood, tears in his eyes, wishing she would drop dead in front of him. It was time she was dead.

The little van drew up beside him.

"Well, there, now, then," said Jones the Milk, who always seemed to use the oddest kind of words when he spoke English. "Having trouble with Cariad, yes?"

"She got out and . . ." Martin had never decided how to speak of the new man in his mother's life to people outside the family. Inside he just said "he".

"He made me go and get her." No need to say that Martin himself was responsible for her straying. She had run faster than he believed possible and turned out of the farm lane on to the road.

She had been glad enough, at first, to see even Martin, when he finally caught up with her. He had lived on the farm for almost six months now. Since she wandered the yard and came into the kitchen if she felt like it, his smell was familiar. Though she usually sensed that he was more of an enemy than a friend, she knew him.

"Hand reared. Bottle fed. They're always greedy and spoiled," Jones the Milk said. Everybody seemed to be called Jones. There was Jones the Post and Jones Ty Gwyn and Jones the Kennels. Or they were called Williams, or Hughes.

Martin's name was Slater and nobody was going to adopt him and change it to Hughes. The Man's name was Gwyn Hughes. They called him Gwyn Bryn Gwynt, which was the name of the farm. It meant Windy Hill and if ever a name was well deserved that was. The wind fought and screamed around the house on three days out of every four and sang in the electricity wires like a screeching banshee.

"Well, now then, let's see. Give her bread, boy," Jones the Milk said. "A hungry creature will do anything for food."

He fished a large bread roll out of a bag beside him. He jumped out of the van, a lean small man with laughing eyes.

Jones the Milk was very little taller than Martin. His bearded face grinned. He was always laughing and he talked to Martin as if he were grown up.

"Well, now then. You can lead a sheep home but you can't make her come," the milkman said.

He held out a piece of the bread roll. Cariad's head swung round and her ears pointed. Her small eyes glittered with desire. Here was a human who understood her. Unexpectedly, she charged, eager to get at the food. Her hard head caught him in the midriff and Jones the Milk fell backwards against his van.

He laughed as he righted himself. "Well, now then. There's trouble for you," he said. "There's how you don't do it," he went on. "Come on, lad. I'll hold her and you run down the road and hold out the next piece of bread and I'll let her go."

It seemed a daft way to carry on. They were all daft here. It was becoming an overused word. Martin did as he was told, not recognizing that this was something he rarely did for anyone at all these days. He ran a hundred yards towards the farm, turned round, held out the bread and whistled.

The ewe trotted purposefully towards him.

Jones the Milk climbed into his van and drove a

little way along the road, stopping beside Cariad. She didn't mind him or the van. He often came to the farm for a cup of tea and a chat, as he lived by himself in one of the farm cottages, away down the lane. The Girls speculated as to which of the many village women that he took out would finally become his wife.

He climbed out of the van and held Cariad again, his fingers buried in her thick fleece. It took four runs to get to the farm gate. Martin did not notice that his mother and Gwyn had been watching him. They turned and went indoors before he arrived.

"There now," Jones the Milk said with satisfaction, as they closed the gate on Cariad. "I'll be on my way or Megan the Lump will be on at me."

Martin had thought that Megan got her name because she was fat, but she was a very thin and a very old lady, who lived in a little cottage beside an enormous rocky outcrop that everyone called the Lump when they spoke English. Martin couldn't pronounce its Welsh name and didn't intend to try.

He turned to face the farmhouse. It was a large building, with more rooms than any house he had ever seen before. It wasn't home. It never would be home, though the Man had given him a room of his own with a desk and a shelf for his books and a worktable where he could make model aeroplanes, and his own black and white TV.

14

"Tell your Da and Mam I'll be calling in a favour," Jones the Milk said, as he climbed into his seat in the van. He favoured Martin with the big grin that showed uneven white teeth with a gap in the front. "For helping with Cariad. A cup of tea and maybe a duck egg or two."

Martin was sure that duck eggs were dangerous to eat. They had salmonella, worse than chickens' eggs. The papers said so.

"All right if you boil them for fifteen minutes," the Man said, when Martin refused to eat his breakfast egg. "And my chickens are safe. We don't use manufactured food here for anything. Do things the old way, the proper way." Martin listened, and ate the egg, but didn't answer. He refused to speak to the Man.

He watched Jones the Milk drive off, with a last wave of his hand. Taid's two collies, Meg and Bryn, were lying in the yard, watching.

"I'm never going to like living in Anglesey," Martin thought, as Cariad trotted across the cobbled yard and butted hopefully at the door. In her view it ought to open at once and reward her with some goodie that was extra tasty to eat.

He was very careful, this time, to latch the heavy five-barred gate behind him. The kitchen door was shut. The ewe, remembering the bread, came to Martin and nosed his hand. Aware of eyes behind the curtains, though not sure whose, he pushed her gently away. He would have liked to thump her.

He went through the kitchen door. In all the time he had lived there he had never seen anyone come in at the front door. He wasn't even sure it would open.

He walked into the tag end of what had evidently been a longstanding discussion. His battle with the ewe had made him hungry. He washed his hands at the sink and looked at his mother. She was sitting at the end of the table with a pad in front of her and a pen in her hand.

She put it away as Martin came in. He felt, as he so often did now, as if he were intruding. She was excluding him from a conspiracy. The others knew about it and he didn't. Nobody wanted him there.

She nodded at the plate on the dresser, filled with Cornish pasties. Nobody ever seemed to stop work in lambing time. The Man came in and out at odd intervals, snatched a sandwich or a pie or a pasty and a flask and was off again. Everyone seemed to eat on the run.

The younger girl, Anna Wyn, was holding a bottle for a young lamb that tugged vigorously at the teat. His small tail circled like a windmill. Anna Wyn seemed either to have a bottle in her hand or a lamb under her arm whenever Martin saw her.

They had only been here a few weeks when the first lamb came, just before Christmas. Surprisingly the press came too. Photographers took pictures of the two girls holding lambs, or bottle feeding them. They tried to make Martin join in, but he refused, glowering.

After that they ignored him, which made him feel like a ghost who nobody saw. Sometimes he wondered if he were a ghost, which was why it paid to do something so awful they had to take notice, like letting the ewe out into the road.

Unexpectedly and annoyingly, he felt bad about that.

Sometimes he tried to put his thoughts into rhyme. It helped to write them down, even if he did tear them up afterwards so that nobody saw. And even if he did know the rhymes were awful.

He looked across the farmyard. There was a tiny moon, a slim glint with a star beneath it, held in the crescent. Darkness shadowed the rolling land. Night had come while he was fighting the old ewe. He stared out through the window into the shadowy yard.

He finished his pasty and sat on the old settee that had a broken spring and was next in line for his mother's attention. She seemed to have developed all kinds of unexpected skills.

She was a different person here. Always laughing, her eager voice often sounding above the others, as she spilled new ideas. Martin didn't like that at all.

Nobody had time for him. Nobody wanted him. Nobody cared about him. He felt nothing but hatred inside him as he trudged miserably up the winding stairs to bed.

Chapter 2

Martin was aware of a constant atmosphere of suppressed excitement. Every time the girls met, they bubbled over with conversation, but it was always in Welsh. His mother was laughing, engrossed as he had never seen her before. Taid was busy, but Martin had no intention of asking anyone what they were doing, or of trying to join in.

He came home from school one afternoon to find that Dilys had the afternoon free, and everyone was sitting round the kitchen table. They were talking loudly when he came in, throwing words at one another. He intended to slip out of the room and up to his bedroom as quickly as possible. Their discussion was nothing to do with him. He didn't want to know.

18

But his mother had other ideas.

"Sit down, Martin," she said. "We're having a committee meeting. We need ideas, because sheep farming isn't making us a good living. If the farm doesn't do well, all of us will suffer. You sometimes have some very good ideas."

Martin looked at them. What was going on? He sat down at the table. If there wasn't enough money for them all, what would happen? Would he and his mother be sent away? It was the first time he had joined in at all. The first time he had thought about the farm and where the money came from to keep them all. He had refused to remember seeing his mother sit and cry, evening after evening, as she struggled to make the figures in her notebook spin out to cover everything they needed.

He hadn't wanted to remember the bad times. Only the good times.

"No pocket money this week for either of us," his mother often said. The food they had to eat, though adequate, was rarely interesting. There was never money for treats. Sometimes, not even for a bar of chocolate at the end of the week. Just debts, his mother said. And more debts.

Here, the meals were terrific.

"Organic farming is another way ahead," his mother said. They had obviously been talking for a long time before he came in. He felt left out and lost. "We can sell the produce in the farm shop."

"What farm shop?" Martin asked, even more bewildered.

"Taid's been making a shop in the old barn at the edge of the lane. Your father has given Anna Wyn the big field beside it, and we're making a little childrens' zoo, and a playground. It's going to be great fun."

Martin found what he hoped would be a real problem.

"It's too far from the road. Nobody would come down here." He was determined to be awkward.

"They will come if we make it a tourist attraction," his mother said. "Taid is building an assault course to give the little ones something to do. Mothers with small children will come. We won't charge a lot."

She pushed her hair out of her eyes.

"There's so little for them; they get bored on the beach and a lot of people now are worried about pollution in the sea."

Martin had visions of the farm being overrun with tiny boys and girls. He didn't like the idea at all.

"You could help Taid make the obstacles." She smiled at the old man, who was also watching Martin, a considering look on his face, as if he thought it unlikely that the boy would co-operate. "Taid invents too; we'll have one of the best playgrounds for children on the island."

"We've enough of my waifs and strays for a

zoo," Dilys said. "Da always tells us every animal must pay its way."

"Like Cariad, who costs us about ten times what she's worth. She stole Leah's cut-and-come-again cake yesterday afternoon." Anna Wyn spoke as if it were a virtue, not a crime. Everyone but Martin laughed.

"Not a real zoo," Leah said. "We'd better call it a sanctuary, or we'll have to have a licence. That costs around five hundred pounds, and means all kinds of inspections."

"We'll see about the animals." Gwyn was always doubtful at first. "Someone will have to be there all the time, as children chase, and some of them aren't very kind. It might be better to have a very extensive play area, and keep the animals right away."

"Most children are good, if you show them what to do," Anna Wyn said. "They love rabbits and guinea pigs, and we can invite nursery and primary school classes and make it educational as well."

Gwyn still looked dubious. But the Girls would get their own way, Martin thought. They always did.

"Right," said his mother in a brisk voice, continuing a speech he hadn't even heard. "We turn more of the farm over to organic produce. We open up a farm trail and Taid makes the most fantastic childrens' playground."

Her voice was bright with interest and her eyes

21

sparkled.

"Anna Wyn and Dilys and Martin can turn the end field and the little barn into an animal sanctuary. We'll need lots of cages, hutches and enclosures. And I'll have the farm shop and maybe a tea room."

Martin had never heard her speak with so much enthusiasm. "We could do farm holidays too, later on," she went on, excitement in her voice. "When we've enough money to furnish the spare bedrooms. They're a bit too spartan at present."

Gywn laughed.

"I didn't know I was marrying a whirlwind," he said.

"There now." Taid's soft voice held laughter. "More like a tornado, sweeping through the house, isn't it?"

Martin was suddenly aware of a rising temper that threatened to overwhelm him. He wanted to shout at them. To pour scorn on their plans and their ideas. Taking it for granted he would be involved and only too willing to slave for them.

Nobody considered him, ever.

He had no intention of helping in any way at all.

He was tired and he was hungry.

The seething anger had to find an outlet. He stood up. He slammed his fist down on the table.

"None of you ask me if I want to be involved,"

he shouted. Everyone stared at him in astonishment. "You forget me, all the time. I'm just Martin, that awful boy, much too young to be included. Martin who nobody wants. Not even my father wanted me. My mother doesn't want me. She never did. You only put up with me because you can't do anything else."

He felt ashamed of the words as he spoke them, but he was too tired and too angry to stop. "I just sit here and don't belong and you don't want me to belong. I'm Martin the rebel and I'll behave like a devil. You needn't think I'm going to help with a lot of stupid little kids that run around bawling every time they fall over. I hate little kids."

There were tears in his eyes and a desperate feeling inside him that clawed at his chest.

Outside the wind's whistle rose to a high keening, an agony of noise. Martin was afraid that tears would spill over and the lump in his throat would choke him.

He had to escape from the astonished faces that stared at him as if he were some freak that had blown in from outside, flung into the kitchen on the raging wind that rattled the windows and screamed through the trees.

He ran from the room, banging the door behind him.

His mother spoke, but he couldn't distinguish the words. He heard her get up and come upstairs to follow him. He turned the key in his door.

"Martin?" He didn't answer. He had no intention of answering. He lay on his bed, staring at a crack in the ceiling, so hungry that he felt sick.

At last he heard his mother's steps going slowly down the stairs, heard Gwyn's soft voice, questioning, heard the kitchen door shut. He had thought yesterday that he couldn't be more miserable. Now he knew he could.

An uneasy silence washed over the farmhouse. He lay on his bed feeling miserable, knowing he ought not to have raged at everyone. He felt, more and more, as if he didn't belong, as if they all had interests that he couldn't share. He resented his mother's closeness to Gwyn, and even resented the bicycle he had been bought when they married.

It wasn't a present, it was a bribe.

He beat his fists against the pillow, and lay there, wanting to yell, while the moon rode up the sky and the uncaring stars stared coldly through his window.

He would never fit in, never, and he wasn't going to try.

Chapter 3

Nobody said anything about his outburst. Martin wished they would. They continued with their plans. Taid vanished into the barn daily, and the sound of hammering could be heard for miles. Anna Wyn spent every spare moment with him. His mother spent hours on mysterious errands. The family happiness had gone. Martin's misery blackened everyone's mood and took the edge off their enjoyment.

He found new ways of being annoying. It was never wise to interfere with the animals. He always had to remedy his misdeeds. The day he let five sheep into the kitchen garden he had to get them back into the field again. It took the whole of one Saturday.

Then a series of events started that had nothing

to do with him at all. The culmination came at half-term. Again Martin was entirely blameless, as he had been the last time it had happened, when he had let Cariad out. And again nobody believed him.

This time even Taid was angry. It was his milk. The bottle was again on its side. The telltale spillage lay across the yard.

"Why, boy, why? So silly, it is," Taid said, his feathery white hair on end, so that Martin thought he looked like a rumpled cockerel. "No point."

"It wasn't me. Maybe it was Cariad."

"Not out of her shed yet, Bach. No use lying." Taid walked away, as if he couldn't bear to look at Martin any longer.

"You'll cycle to the village and get Taid more milk. And pay for both bottles yourself." His step-father revealed unusual impatience in his voice. "When you come back it's clean out Cariad's bed and put fresh straw in for her. Time you stopped your nonsense, boy."

They never used his name when they were annoyed with him. His mother looked at him with tight lips and unhappy eyes, but said nothing. He knew that she was angrier than either of the men.

Martin wheeled his bike out into the lane. He closed the gate carefully behind him, making an operation of it, so that everyone would notice. It wasn't fair. This time he was as innocent as the

26

newborn ewe lamb that was struggling on rubbery legs to suckle from her mother in the field beside the gate.

He had no intention of hurrying. In any case it was another pig of a day, with a wild wind whirling sodden clouds. When he turned down the road that led to the beach, only a short distance from the Sea Zoo, surly waves crashed against the splintered rock in a smother of foam.

He stood, rain beating against his face and soaking his hair. Across the Straits the houses of Port Dinorwic huddled together. Further down he could see the giant tanks at Caernarfon. A bedraggled oyster catcher poked dispiritedly in the wet sand just showing at the edge of the tide.

He ought to have cycled along the main road and then hurried back. The wind here was fierce. Gales in the Irish Sea. There were always gales in the Irish Sea. He pushed his bicycle along the wet road. The gusts were too strong for him to ride and he regretted his decision to take the long way round, and make Taid wait for his milk.

He knew his mother would lend some to the old man. The delay would make no difference. But he'd take his time all the same. They could all wait. It was all their fault. They should have believed him.

Maybe Cariad had got out and then put herself back. He wouldn't put it past her. He wouldn't put anything past her. Maybe Taid knocked over the milk bottle and spilled the milk himself. He was old and old people were forgetful.

But Martin knew Taid wouldn't have knocked over his own milk. Not three mornings running.

There was a man playing with a dog on the beach. An enormous dog that cavorted happily at the edge of the tide, its mouth agape with joy. An Alsatian. They were fierce, Martin was sure.

He prayed that the dog wouldn't see him, wouldn't come near, wouldn't leave the edge of the sea. The man called the dog, and held it as the boy pushed his cycle past them. Suppose the dog ran after him? Suppose it bit him? Martin tried to ride, but the wind forced him off again.

The entrance to the Sea Zoo offered sanctuary. If he went in and dallied long enough, maybe the man and the dog would have gone when he came out. He could see the man's car parked in the rough grass. Surely it was too wet and windy to stay on the beach for long?

He would have liked to call in at the Zoo itself and walk through the quiet passages among the tanks full of gliding fish. To stand on the heavy timber bridge and watch the giant flatfish come up and gulp at the air. To marvel at the way they became invisible whether on shingle or sand, their chameleon colours matching and blending so it was only just possible to see them.

He had been to the Sea Zoo only once before. The wreck room had enchanted him. It had felt as if he were in an old galleon sunk at the bottom

28

of the sea. Above him fish swam, and all around him, and he sat on the rotting steps and felt peace sweep into his mind. It was dark and soothing and he was the only visitor that day. The wave room was terrific. The water built up in the tank, and then swept with a crash and thunder and swirl along, and out at the back to fall in cascades in the next room. Stand too near and the spray soaked you. Martin spent over an hour there, fascinated by the surge and roar and riotous power behind the immense green rollers.

Time stopped, or maybe swept him back into a kinder age. He didn't know. Now he hadn't enough money to go in, but he did have enough to buy a small tub of food for the trout in the big ponds beside the shop. The man behind the counter of the Catch and Carry fish stall smiled at him, and he felt soothed.

He scattered the food over the water and watched the sudden boil as the trout surfaced, excited mouths grabbing. Then all was still again, the water hiding hundreds of lithe bodies. It must be nice to be a fish.

"Nasty day, son," the big man on the fish counter said as he passed. Martin nodded, and almost smiled. Nobody here blamed him or threatened him. Nobody knew who he was. It was good to be anonymous.

Once away from the shore he was able to cycle between the trees that shrouded the long lane. Past the pottery that opened to the public in summer, past the police house, and then past the pub on the corner and back to the store where he collected milk in cardboard cartons that would be less likely to come to harm if he fell from his bike. He tucked them in the saddle bag. If Taid's milk was delivered in cartons it wouldn't spill when it was knocked over.

Back at the farm everyone was busy, with no time for him. Another of the ewes had given birth the day before and the whole family were hanging over the fence, staring at her lamb.

Martin, glancing across, saw why they were looking. The little animal's rear end was swollen, like a huge woolly balloon, although she was sucking and lively.

"Never seen anything like that before," Taid said. "Not in all the years on the farm. Vet for her, isn't it?"

Gwyn lifted the little animal and put her in the back of his Land Rover. The ewe bawled her misery at losing her baby. Martin's mother took her and put her in the barn, where her deep sorrowing bleats echoed throughout the day.

Gwyn was not home till late afternoon.

Martin had cleaned the shed, and given Taid his milk.

"No apology, boy?" Taid asked, just before tea.

"I didn't do it." Martin's voice was sullen.

He had no intention of apologizing for something that wasn't his fault. The sound of the

Land Rover in the yard saved him from Taid's reply.

Gwyn began to speak rapidly to his father in Welsh and then seeing Martin watching, changed to English.

"No back passage, the little one. Just sealed up. Matt tried to operate, but there was nothing there. Put to sleep. Dai Plas Eryri has a new orphan. Needs skinning, Taid."

Martin couldn't believe his ears. Skinning? Were they going to use her for meat? He would never eat lamb again. The lambs always went away for butchering. Martin didn't like the thought of that either, but nobody else seemed to mind.

He went indoors and up to his room, and lay on his bed, hating the world. He tuned his radio and put on the headphones. No noise, his mother said. No noise at all. He wanted the crashing chords to blare out and drown every other sound on the farm. He wanted the music to beat into his head. To stop him thinking.

That was no good. He went downstairs again.

He wasn't interested in sheep. He would never be interested in sheep. For all that, he couldn't get the lamb out of his head. It had been so alive. Running around, enjoying herself. And then, dead, because she had been born malformed. Only half made, Anna Wyn had said. Everything inside her in the wrong place or not there at all. Yet she had been able to run and feed.

The ewe was still bleating, sorrowing for her

31

lost baby. Did his mother ever feel that about him? If he ran away, would she grieve or would she just be relieved that he had gone? He wished he could control his thoughts. These didn't belong in his head at all, nor did the niggling sympathy for the ewe and the pity for the little lamb that had only lived a few hours.

Everyone was busy. He could be busy too but he didn't intend to help. Anna Wyn was feeding two orphaned kittens that had been found in a ditch, with no mother anywhere to account for them. Jones the Milk had heard them crying and brought them in that morning. They were only a couple of weeks old.

She was using a syringe to drip milk into the tiny mouths. They were so small and helpless that Martin felt a tug of pity and interest that he refused to acknowledge.

Daft to spend so much time on creatures like that. Too many animals in the world anyway.

Anna Wyn didn't look up. The black mite had its front paws wrapped round her hand, and its back paws flexed as it fed. It was unbelievably small.

Martin's mother was equally busy with a lamb and a bottle. Taid and his stepfather were in the lambing barn. Curious, Martin looked through the door and was startled to see a tiny black-nosed, black-legged lamb wearing the dead lamb's coat, which was far to big for it. Taid was busy tacking it on with big stitches.

Neither man had noticed him. They were talking in rapid Welsh. Gwyn seemed to be telling his father something, but Taid was talking to the frightened lamb. One of the big grey farm cats sat on a bale of straw, his green eyes watching.

Behind Martin a motor revved and then died away. He turned to see Sam the Hounds carrying a heavy lumpy plastic bin liner into his van. A stately Golden Retriever sat in the passenger seat of the van, his eyes watchful. Sam waved and drove off. It seemed to be a known routine. So the dead lamb was fed to the Hunt pack.

The wind had died and the rain given way to a watery sky, patched with gold where the sun shone through. Martin watched as his stepfather carried the strange lamb over to the ewe. She stopped her mournful noise and sniffed the lamb. It bleated, a small tentative baaing sound. It was very young.

She butted it away.

Taid shook salt on to the lamb's head. He took straw from the floor and rubbed it over the lamb's coat, and then, while Gwyn held the ewe, Taid put the baby to suck.

The ewe licked at the small head. She was a large beast and he was tiny. Gwyn's flock were Texels. Martin knew that.

"Pity the baby had to be a Suffolk," Taid said. "Have to take what God sends us." He had seen Martin watching. Martin wondered why it mattered. Cariad was a Suffolk too. The Texels

33

were big grey sheep. The Suffolks had black faces and black legs and were small and chunky.

"She's taking to him, but we had better keep them in for at least a week." Gwyn patted the ewe on the head. "There then, he's yours now. Take care of him."

They closed the door. Martin realized how aware he had been of her pitiful bleating, as she mourned for her lost lamb. He was glad that it had stopped. He wanted to ask if many were born deformed in that way and why it happened?

"It's a shame," his mother said. "I hope there aren't any more like that." She dished out the casserole that had been cooking slowly in the Aga.

"Four hundred sheep," Anna Wyn said, tossing her long blonde hair away from her eyes. "We always lose a few."

"And always sorry," said Taid. "Losing a life. That's a bad thing. Bringing in new life. Nothing like it." He chewed thoughtfully. It had been many days since he went home for his meals. "You dont get used to it, but you accept it . . . nothing else to do. Part of living."

Martin thought of the lamb when he was in bed. Life seemed suddenly precarious, an enormous risk. Life here was what mattered to everyone. Keeping the kittens from dying; keeping the injured buzzard in the bird shed from giving up the struggle for existence. His broken wing was splinted. He was a pathetic looking bird,

34

as miserable as the turkey that had suddenly developed pneumonia.

Martin had never realized a bird could look so dejected. Taid fed him anti-biotics for three days and now he was in hospital at the vet's. A turkey hospital. How daft could you get?

He was almost asleep when fear hit him. Suppose Taid's milk was upset tomorrow morning. They'd have the same misery all over again. He knew he couldn't bear to be wrongly accused next time. He would have to try not to do such stupid things, or they would blame him for everything that went wrong.

They hadn't been furious with him; only sad. Nobody shouted at him, or slapped him, or shook him. Taid looked disappointed and his stepfather looked grim, but then he had been grim all this week, up at night lambing.

Martin heard him dress and go downstairs three or four times every night, looking over the ewes.

"Have a television to watch them when my ship comes home," Gwyn said, each morning, rubbing red rimmed eyes and a bristly jaw, and yawning. "And a big lambing shed, not the old barn and straw bales all round them. Makes so much work." Martin drifted off into sleep.

He woke to hear a rapping on his bedroom door. He glanced at his clock. Only 6 a.m. What on earth did Gwyn want with him?

"Get up, boy, quick, and come downstairs. Don't make a noise."

Startled, and also alarmed, Martin began to dress, an immense worry making his fingers clumsy. Was his mother ill? What was happening out there in the yard? Had she gone to help with the lambs and slipped and fallen on ice?

"I'm sorry," Gwyn said. "Shouldn't have blamed you. Look."

He lifted the curtain. The light spilled from the window and shadowed the yard. There at Taid's door where Jones the Milk had left the bottle early, was some animal. It had knocked over the bottle and was lapping hungrily at the spill on the ground.

"A stray dog," Gwyn said. "We need to catch him, or he'll be after our lambs next. Someone must have dumped him. He isn't local. Saw him as I came out of the barn. He bolted and hid, but as soon as I came in he was back. Starving, I shouldn't wonder."

"How will you catch him?" Martin asked. He was glad he wasn't outside. The dog was an Alsatian, thin as any animal could be, harsh fur lying soaked against his ribby body. He glanced around him fearfully, even while he drank. "Get some dope from the vet to put in his food once he begins to trust us. Terrified, poor brute," Gwyn said, pity in his voice. He hated any harm coming to any animal, even to a dog that might raid his lamb field. "Put food down by the milk bottles tomorrow; and maybe then Taid will keep his milk."

"I'll get Taid more," Martin said, forgetting it was a schoolday. He was so relieved to find that at last they believed him.

"Not to worry, boy." Gwyn squeezed Martin's shoulder, asking his forgiveness without words, acknowledging that his stepson had tried to make amends. "Your mother's going shopping this morning. Taid can have some of ours till then. Maybe we ought to get a cow; though milking her would be another chore. So busy, always."

Martin had to run for the school bus. Climbing in, he sat, as he always did, at the back, trying not to feel alone. He imagined himself earning enough money to buy a cow and learning to milk her and the family approving and agreeing that maybe he wasn't so bad after all.

The pleasure that thought gave him lasted until he got to school and remembered that the first lesson would be Welsh and that he still hadn't managed to learn anything, though last night he had tried to do some homework. The words just wouldn't stay in his mind.

He nerved himself to endure another day.

Chapter 4

A bright Saturday, and the weekend ahead. Martin woke early and looked out of his window. The mountains loomed stark and black against the sky, which promised rain later. On fine days they were softer shapes, masked by haze. They were always different, so that even he was now beginning to be weatherwise.

Faint cloud masked the tops. It would build and bring torrents before nightfall.

He had overslept. Everyone was busy. No one had bothered about him. He had his own weekend chores but they weren't important. They could be done at any time during the morning.

Resentment flickered. They didn't trust him with anything important. They never asked him for help. They were all against him, even his mother. She cooked them breakfast. She had left cornflakes and cold toast out for him. Why couldn't she have woken him? She just didn't care.

He ate quickly, tasting nothing, seething with irritation. There was no outlet. He knew better than to try any more mischief. In any case, it didn't work. It only left him with more to do, as he had to remedy every mistake himself. Taid was cleaning his doorstep. The morning intruder had been and gone, leaving the bottle of milk overturned as usual.

"Let him drink," Taid said, when he had been told what was causing the trouble. "Starving, he'll be. Food might tame him."

They had continued the conversation at supper-time.

"Need to catch him," Taid said. "Can't do it yet. He's wary. Off like a flash of lightning if we go near."

"And then?" Martin's mother asked.

"The Dog's Home, " Gwyn said. "Or the RSPCA."

"They'll put him down if nobody claims him," Anna Wyn said. "And nobody will. Or they'd have been looking. I've asked around."

"Can't have a dog running free with our sheep." Gwyn stood up, spooned sugar into his coffee, drank, and left the table. There was a ewe due to lamb, and he expected problems.

"Especially a German Shepherd," he added,

as he went out of the door and shut it gently behind him.

"I thought it was an Alsatian," Martin said.

"It's the same dog. They changed the name from German Shepherd to Alsatian when we were fighting the Germans. Now we aren't, they've changed it back. They were used for sheep; still are in some places."

Martin couldn't get the dog out of his mind. It had looked such a pathetic animal; frightened, scrawny, nervous, checking all the time it drank. The pointed ears flickered, the head turned from side to side, the desperate eyes watching for danger. It must be young as it was much smaller than the big dogs of the same breed that lived in the village.

Poor dog. He didn't like dogs at all but the thought of it worried him. Unwanted, unfed, roaming, hunting to keep itself alive. It was worse off than Martin himself. At least he had food and shelter, even if nobody cared about him at all.

By mid-morning, everyone had gone out. Gwyn had promised them lunch at the local pub, *The Setters*, as it was Anna Wyn's birthday. Martin refused to go.

"Martin, please," his mother said. ·

"I don't want to come. It's nothing to do with me. I want to stay here."

He avoided her eyes as she looked at him. He knew he was distressing her, and was glad.

Maybe now she'd think about him a bit more. She'd bought Anna Wyn a dress to wear when she went to the disco last week. She never bought him a decent present.

He didn't want to remember that Gwyn had given him a new bike; or that he had had more Christmas presents than ever before in his life. Or that he had not yet had a birthday. That wasn't due till the end of July. Months ahead.

He watched them drive away, looking out of his bedroom window. He half hoped they might stop and come back and ask him to think again. But nobody did.

The farmhouse was empty, except for the cats. Martin had never been left on his own before. He prowled uneasily from room to room.

The bad weather he'd predicted earlier in the morning had now arrived with a vengeance. Wind swept through the trees, screeched in the wires and rattled the loose corners of the old barn.

Rain drove out of a sombre sky, lancelike drops dancing on the worn cobbles. Rain lashed mercilessly against the windows. Rain beat down remorselessly on the fields so that the sheep huddled in the shelter of the hedges, forlorn and soaking. Martin couldn't stay indoors. There was a restlessness inside him, a desire to ride for miles on his bike, or to run against the wind. It was no use even trying to cycle today. He couldn't ride. Gale Force, the weather forecast had said. Rising to Force 11 in the Irish Sea.

You couldn't even stand in the gusts at that wind strength.

It was a wild and wicked day.

If only it were fine. He had been looking forward to the weekend. But it wasn't fine and he had to make what he could of it. The screaming of the wind produced an uneasiness inside him. The creaking branches of the trees threatened him. Suppose one of them fell? Suppose the giant sycamore behind the barn was torn out by the roots? There were animals in the barn.

Not even he could let them die. Martin wondered if he ought to move them. He wondered if the tree were really safe. He stared at it through the rainstreaked glass. Although the branches bowed and twisted it seemed steady enough.

He could walk round the farm, and check the animals. He would pretend he wasn't. The last thing he wanted was to take care of any of the stock, but a niggling feeling of responsibility left him aware that nobody but he could deal with any emergency today. Did they trust him enough to leave him the care of the farm?

"Lock up if you go out." That was all Gwyn had said as they left.

And he did have to go out. To do something, to walk the fields, climb the stiles, brave the wind and the rain.

He locked the back door and hid the key under the bale in the yard, in case the rest of the family came home earlier than he expected.

Through the gate past the duckpond. Not even the ducks were out today. They were foraging in the barn.

Cariad pushed at him, nosing his hand. She never worried about rain, especially if she thought there was likely to be food around.

"Get off, you silly beast," Martin said, and she stood, disconsolate, and watched him as he opened the gate that led into the first field. He closed it behind him carefully. He was trying to remember all that Gwyn had told him, but it was easy to forget.

Some of his sins were accidents, not deliberate, as everyone thought.

The river was running fast and peaty brown. Soon it would be overflowing, spilling into the fields, making a lake where none had been before. Gwyn, mindful always of the weather, had shifted all the sheep to the higher ground. Only the lambing ewes and the orphan lambs were in the barn.

The farm and its outbuildings stood high, well above the level of even the most severe floods.

Martin kept away from the banks, which were slippery with mud. Two men had drowned while fishing last year. He was aware of danger everywhere.

The path wound up the hill to the top field and a little copse that sheltered so many wild animals. There was a vixen. Gwyn had seen her one morning, a hare in her mouth, racing towards the shelter of the bushes. He told them at breakfast. Soon there would be cubs. Dilys said there were badgers, and Martin often saw the hunting owl.

The wind noise reminded Martin of a child screaming. Oddly, the sounds were not all around him. They seemed to be coming from further up the hill.

A moment later he realized a child was screaming, an impassioned hopeless sobbing interrupting the yells.

He ran, braving the wind that forced itself against him, and blew into his face, so that it was difficult to breathe. Along the path, panting as he ran. Along the fence that bordered the trees. Round the corner of the wood, his side hurting. He had a stitch, a sharp pain in his chest. Last year's dead brambles tugged at his legs and scratched his hands.

Up ahead there was a splash of red lying on the ground just beside the wall.

Martin stopped, afraid that whatever lay there was covered in blood. Then he realized he was looking at clothing. A moment later he stared down at a fair-haired child, trapped under the tumbled stones.

The wall had collapsed. Martin tried to shift the rocks, but they were much too heavy. The boy's arm was pinned beneath them. Maybe broken.

"It's all right," Martin said, kneeling beside the child, trying to attract his attention. He was sobbing so hard that he could barely see out of his swollen eyes.

The child took a deep breath.

"It hurts." The words were barely distinguishable among the sobs.

"Can you pull your arm out?" Martin asked. "If I pull you?"

"No. I can't breathe properly. The rocks are so heavy. I think my arm's broken. It hurts so much."

Martin tried again to shift one of the stones, but that only produced another fall. If he weren't careful a boulder might roll on to the child's head. Martin had never realized how precarious the walls were, made without anything but their own weight to keep the rocks in place.

He looked down at the child. He was such a little boy. He must have been trying to climb the wall.

"Look," Martin said, not knowing what to do. "I'll have to get help. I'll be quick as I can, OK? Can you hang on without being too frightened? Someone will come, as quick as I can get them, I promise. I can't stay with you, or nobody will know."

"I'll be all right, now I know somebody knows," the small boy said. He wiped his free arm across his face, smearing the tears.

Martin unzipped his anorak and folded it under the child's head. He had to do something to try to make the little boy feel more comfortable.

45

He raced down the hill, slipping and sliding on the wet grass. Rain soaked him. The wind tore at his hair and bit through his clothes. He slowed to a fast walk. No use breaking his own leg. That would make two of them in trouble.

He grabbed the key from under the bale, unlocked the door and burst into the kitchen.

Gwyn's notebook lay by the telephone. It listed the numbers of the vet, the doctor, and of their immediate neighbours. He dialled two of the neighbouring farms. Nobody was at home. He thought hard. Something had to be done, and done fast. The child was soaked and must be suffering from shock and shock was dangerous. Martin knew that climbers on the mountain often died of exposure to the wind and rain and cold rather than from their injuries.

Panic dried his throat. He dialled 999, hoping the police wouldn't think it a hoax. Boys did play hoaxes, and he might not be believed. He explained rapidly to the man who answered his call.

"Slow down, son," said the voice at the other end of the line. "Tell me again. Is it your brother?"

"I don't know who he is. He's very little. I'm all alone. Everyone's gone out. I'm not big enough to move the stones. I tried, but they began to slip more and I thought I'd hurt him worse." Martin felt as if he were falling over his tongue in his effort to explain. Suppose the child was really badly hurt and died? It would be dreadful to die up there, all alone, nobody near him to comfort him or hold his hand.

"Someone'll be with you soon," the voice said, re-assuring. "Stay by the farmhouse so that you can guide them across the fields. OK?"

"OK," Martin said.

He looked at the clock. The minute hand seemed to have slowed to a standstill. It crept round, second by eternal second. They were never going to come. They hadn't believed him. They couldn't find the farm. It was remote enough, heaven knew. A stupid place to live. In the town everyone could find a house quickly. Here, if he had an accident, he could die and nobody would know until they all came home.

And then another thought struck him. If he had gone out with the family he wouldn't have walked up the hill. He wouldn't have found the little boy. The child might have died there, with nobody finding him until it was too late.

His grandmother always said that things were meant to happen in a certain way; and that one thing led to another, always unexpectedly.

The wind rose to a crescendo, savaging the trees. It drowned the engine of the approaching car. The sharp rat-tat tat on the door made Martin jump.

"We've rung for an ambulance," the man said.

"Will you take us to the child and then come back to show the men where to come? I should think he'll need a stretcher." Martin stared at him. He was used to the mountain rescue helicopter flying over the house. He had never thought of men climbing the wild hills, dragging themselves up rocks, to manhandle an injured man down the steep slopes.

There was no time to think of that now. He set off at a swift pace through the yard, opening the gate for the two men.

One of them shut it behind them. They climbed through the huddled sheep, until, after endless minutes, they came out on the top path, beside the little wood.

"Well now, Bach, you are in a mess," one of the men said, and bent down to look at the little boy. "We'll soon have those stones off you. Have to be careful, though. Don't want more of the wall tumbling down, do we?"

"Back to the house, boy, for the ambulance," the other man said to Martin. "Slowly, now. We don't want another casualty."

The ambulance pulled into the yard as Martin reached the gate. He was out of breath, and for the moment unable to talk. The two men came towards him.

"Take it easy, son," one of them said. "Up in the fields, is he? A tractor accident, is it?"

Martin shook his head, wondering if anyone would drive a tractor on such a day. The wind was

48

increasing in strength, driving against him so that it was hard to stand. Heads down, they followed the path through the fields again, Martin's legs protesting as he tried to walk fast for the third time.

He would dream of running through those fields and of the wind and rain blinding him. He had forgotten to put on another anorak and he was soaked. Rain plastered his hair against his head and ran down into his eyes. They were walking into the wind. It punched the strength from him.

The child was lying clear of the wall, with a police greatcoat cuddled round him. His eyes were closed. Martin could hear his chattering teeth in the lulls of the wind.

The ambulance men stripped the child fast and rolled him in blankets. They put a rainproof cover over them, and set off at an astoundingly fast pace towards the farmyard. Suddenly Martin's teeth began to chatter too.

"Back as fast as we can, boy, and into the bath with you. No use courting pneumonia." A heavy police coat was draped around him, and each man took one of his hands.

"Moving will warm you."

The Welsh voice was matter of fact.

It wasn't so easy to walk fast. Martin felt as if his legs would never work again. They ached all over. He put one foot in front of the other, and plodded on, thankful for the strong arms that helped him over the tricky places. The hill sloped steeply up to the wood. It was good to plunge downhill.

The farmhouse kitchen was warm and welcoming. Sooty, one of Dilys' kittnes, came to rub herself against his legs and then shook herself, disgusted by the wet.

"Off with those clothes fast. Into the bath and into dry clothes. We'll make a hot drink down here. Family due back soon?"

Martin nodded. He was too tired to explain.

"All right on your own?"

He nodded again. He shivered as he ran the water, but lying in the bath, he felt the cold drain away. He wanted to lie there for ever, but he dried himself fast. He put on clean jeans and a thick jersey.

The two policemen had foraged in the cupboards and found instant soup. A steaming mug stood on the table.

The older man, burly, with dark hair touched with grey, sat in Taid's chair, Sweep on his knee, purring as he rubbed behind its ears. The other man was standing with his back to the Aga, warming himself.

"Will the little boy be all right?" Martin asked, halfway through his mug of soup.

"Maybe a broken arm. The rocks weren't crushing him, just trapping him. Very lucky, he was. And lucky anyone found him at all, on such a wild day. Wouldn't have caught me going for a walk today, up that hill." The younger man was smiling.

"I didn't know what to do with myself," Martin said. "I needed a walk. That seemed the best way to go."

"Lucky indeed. Seems it's the little American boy from the caravan at Price Evans the Nursery. Tag, they all call him. Tags along after everyone, like. His sister is older. A lot older. Seems she was in charge of him."

"How do you know?" Martin asked.

"Radio, boy. Wonderful invention." The man in the chair chuckled, and patted his walkie talkie. "Had a long talk while you were bathing. The ambulance men found out his name and where he lived. They rang his home from the police station. Only the girl at home and her worried out of her mind. She's been looking for him for two hours. Her parents went out, see."

So he wasn't the only one that forgot, Martin thought. He felt very sorry for the girl, but oddly glad that others too could make mistakes. It made all his seem less terrible.

The wind had grown to hurricane force. Its shrieks drowned the sound of the returning Land Rover. Martin turned his head as the kitchen door was flung wide open, and Gwyn erupted into the room, his eyes angry.

"Now what's been going on here?" he demanded. "Can't leave you alone a minute, boy, without something happening. What have you done to bring the police here?"

Martin stared at him. Tears filled his eyes. It wasn't fair. Whatever he did was wrong, and now, once more, he was being blamed for something that wasn't his fault at all.

Chapter 5

"The boy's done nothing wrong," one of the policemen said hastily. "Bit of a hero, he is."

Martin watched his stepfather's face relax. The rest of the family had piled in behind him, just in time to hear the words.

"Little lad from the caravan at Price Evans the Nursery pulled the stone wall down on him. Your lad found him. Couldn't lift the rocks himself, so he very sensibly called us."

"Is the child all right?" Martin's mother asked.

"Yes. But he wouldn't have been if he hadn't been found and if your lad hadn't used his wits. It's a wicked day to be lying on the hill injured."

"Little Tag. He's an imp of mischief," Dilys said. "He's always in trouble. He's only six now.

Goodness knows what he'll be like when he's older."

"Maybe today's mishap will make him wiser," the younger of the two policemen said. He smiled at Martin and gave him a little wink. "We'll be off. That lad of yours has had a soaking and he'll be tired tomorrow. Up and down that hill about five times in the wind and the rain. Had my legs aching and I only did it once. Needs a good hot meal and an early night, I shouldn't wonder."

"I'm sorry, Martin," Gwyn said when the two policemen had gone. "Not used to finding police cars parked outside the farm, see?"

Martin still felt hurt, but he did understand that his stepfather had good reason for worry. Nobody would think of an accident involving somebody else. Something going wrong on the farm would have been much more probable. Though offhand he couldn't think of anything he was likely to do that would bring a police car.

"You did well, boy," Taid said. "Not everyone would have kept his head."

For all their praise, it was Gwyn's first words as he came into the room that Martin remembered. They came back to niggle at him while he was eating, and later when he lay in bed listening to the wind roaring round the house.

The weather had worsened during the evening. Now there were banshee screams in the trees, and a wild keening. Martin fell asleep, imagining that the whole house was rocking like a ship at sea.

He ached with effort and with misery. They would never trust him at all.

He slept restlessly. His legs ached and dreams tormented him. Dreams in which he was running up an endless hill towards a screaming child that he'd never reach. The screams changed to a continuous howling, a desperate sound that pierced his brain.

He woke to the sound of heavy rain. The forlorn howls were real. The wind had dropped, but lightning still flashed intermittantly across the ceiling, followed immediately by a thunder crash. The storm was too close for comfort.

Martin found new fears to worry him. Suppose lightning struck the house? Everyone else seemed to be asleep. Should he wake them? But that would reveal his own fears. He lay still, listening to the most unearthly noise.

An animal out in the storm? What animal? No sheep ever made a noise like that. Even as he listened an echo came from the farm dogs. A long mournful moaning.

Martin flung on jeans and jersey and ran downstairs. He was scared. But he had to find out what was wrong.

Lightning zig-zagged across the sky and lit the stairs as he ran down them.

Rain now beat on the ground, coming from a sky slashed by forked flashes. The rumble was further away. It echoed from the hills. The storm was receding.

Martin heard the sound again. It seemed to be coming from just outside the back door, where a small porch gave some shelter from the wind. He undid the bolts and turned the key and opened the door.

A lean shape streaked into the kitchen. The cats spat and jumped high. Martin stared, startled, at the thinnest dog he had ever seen in his life. It was soaked to the skin and shivering. As the thunder crashed again it crept across the floor and pressed its wet body against Martin's legs.

Pity for the animal overcame his fear.

"Martin?" It was Anna Wyn's voice. She came into the room, tying her dressing gown belt. "I heard you come down. I can't sleep either. I hate thunder."

She saw the dog.

"That must be Taid's visitor. He's terrified, poor fellow. And what a state he's in. Get a towel and dry him. I'll warm some milk for him. We can't put him out in the storm again."

Martin took a big towel from the press and began to rub the dog dry. The animal did not protest, but continued to shiver. Anna Wyn went to fetch a fan heater, which she turned on.

"That'll help blow him dry."

"Then what do we do?" Martin asked. "If we tell the RSPCA or the Dog's Home they'll put him to sleep." It was suddenly overwhelmingly important that the dog should live. He was real, he was here, and like Martin, he belonged

56

nowhere. Nobody could possibly be afraid of such a pathetic animal. Martin did not even remember that he was scared of dogs.

"Think about that later," Anna Wyn said. "Let's get him warm and dry now."

She put the milk down in a bowl and the dog drank as if he had never fed before.

"He's been living wild for weeks," she said. "Look at his ribs. He's like a streak of light. Looks like a pedigree animal too. I suppose someone just dumped him."

"Here?"

"On the hills. He'd come down to houses, knowing there'd be food there. Here, boy. I wonder what your name is?" She flicked her fingers and the dog crept to her and pushed his head against her hand. "I hate people," Anna Wyn said. "How can they be so cruel?"

Easily, Martin thought, remembering the times he was tormented at school. People weren't kind to each other, and would be far less kind to animals. He felt a sudden rush of protective feeling towards the dog, and for the first time understood how Gwyn and the girls felt about their charges.

The dog had come to him for help. He had been so afraid of the storm that he had braved humans, even though he had probably met nothing but unkindness from them up to now.

"We ought to go back to bed or we'll be good for nothing tomorrow. Perhaps he'll settle in the kitchen," Anna Wyn said. "The cats seem to have the right idea. They're out of reach."

The dog watched them go towards the door. He ran across as Martin opened it, intending to follow the boy. Anna Wyn pushed him back gently and closed the door, only to hear a long mournful howl.

"Look," Martin said. "Stay with him and I'll get my blankets and pillow and sleep on the window seat. He'll wake everyone if he makes that noise. He can't come upstairs. He's got fleas."

Anna Wyn looked at him, one eyebrow raised, but said nothing. She waited with the dog until Martin returned.

The window seat was long and well padded. Both Gwyn and Anna Wyn took turns to sleep there if they had an orphaned animal that needed frequent feeding. There was often a sickly lamb in a box by the Aga. Martin was glad there wasn't one there tonight.

The dog watched Martin lay his blankets and pillow on the seat. His tail waved very slowly from side to side, almost as if he were afraid he would be reprimanded for daring to move. Watchful brown eyes followed Martin round the room. The dog *was* a German Shepherd, as Gwyn had thought. His ears, at the moment, lay flat against his head. Worried eyes looked up at Martin.

His coat was harsh, chestnut on the flanks, white underneath, black on his saddle, with flashes of gold and grey showing through the fur.

"You are a pathetic thing," Martin said, and the long tail waved gently again, very slowly, as if the dog were unsure or had never tried to show pleasure before. Outside the rain eased. The thunder rumbles were more distant. But flashes of light still flared across the sky. Every time the noise sounded, the dog crept closer to Martin and thrust his nose into the boy's side.

At last they both slept.

Chapter 6

Gwyn, coming down in the early dawn, opened the door and switched on the light. The dog streaked across the room, and sat shivering, pressed against the door. Martin woke slowly, shaking his head to clear his eyes.

"He was frightened of the storm," he said, his eyes on his stepfather's face. "Anna Wyn gave him some milk." He was unaware that he had actually used one of the girls' real names. The dog had roused the strangest feelings in him. He wanted it to stay; he wanted to look after it. He wanted something of his own.

"Needs flea spray," Gwyn said, as he looked down at the animal. "I hope he's not left us too many unwanted visitors." He glanced up at the cats who still sat side by side like statues on top of the dresser. Neither wanted to risk the floor. They knew about dogs.

Gwyn looked at them and shook his head.

"Plenty of sense, cats. We'll feed him and then when the office opens, I'll ring the RSPCA. Good thinking to catch him, boy."

"I want to keep him. For my own," Martin said. He looked up at his stepfather, willing Gwyn to say yes, although he knew it was most unlikely. Of all the dogs in the world, Gwyn thought the German Shepherd the least trustworthy.

Martin made a small bargain with God. If he lets me keep him I'll try to belong. That wasn't enough. He added a postscript, wondering if God would listen, would care. If Gwyn sends him away, I won't try, ever. I want this dog. He needs me. I need him. He came to me, of his own free will. Martin went on talking inside his head. The words wouldn't come out.

"Go up and wash and dress, boy. We'll talk about it at breakfast. Right?"

His stepfather hadn't said yes, but he hadn't said no. As Martin went out of the room the dog ran to the door and began to whimper. Gwyn soothed the animal.

Martin had never dressed so quickly in his life. He wanted the dog so passionately that he couldn't even understand himself. No animal had ever trusted him before. The sheep were wary, always, of people, except for Gwyn and Anna Wyn. Cariad pestered everyone, only wanting

61

food. He hated the geese, who were apt at times to chase. The farm dogs belonged to Gwyn and Taid's dogs had little time for anyone but their master.

Martin didn't like dogs. He didn't like animals. But this dog begged to be his. It felt as if he had been waiting for Martin to come along. He ran back down the stairs to the kitchen.

Taid, summoned by the smell of cooking bacon, looked at the German Shepherd.

"So that's the villain, is it?" he said. "Nothing much to fear there. Not sixpennyworth of him, and only a baby too. Maybe seven months old. Not more."

"He can't go to the Dog's Home," Dilys said. "I'll take him in to surgery with me. They can kennel him and we'll find him a home. Poor fellow. He needs feeding up, and teaching that people are kind. Someone's going to have a hard task."

"Gentle enough," Martin's mother said.

The dog had come to sit beside Martin, leaning against his knee. He watched anxiously as people moved, and flinched when they came too near. He monitored every movement, his eyes following each hand on its way to put the food in the mouth.

"I want him," Martin said. He couldn't eat his breakfast. He felt sick with anxiety. If Gwyn said no it would be the end of the world. He must have the dog. Please, God, please. I'll try and be good for ever if only he lets me keep him.

Everyone was staring at him. Martin wanting a dog. Nobody could believe it. He always avoided the farm collies and Taid's two retired sheepdogs. His mother looked at him, a slight frown on her face.

"Martin, are you sure? A dog like that . . . we don't know his history, or his breeding. He could grow up into a ruffian; chase the sheep . . . who's going to train him?"

"I am. Taid will teach me."

Taid looked across the table, his eyebrows rising into his white hair.

"Only trained sheepdogs, boy. Not Alsatians."

"Why can't he learn to herd sheep?"

"Doubt if he can learn anything, the start he's had." Taid's voice was regretful. "Perhaps the police dog handlers will help me." Martin was desperate.

"He chose me," he added.

The dog stood up slowly and stretched himself. He looked up at Martin as if he had understood that they were talking about him. He sat, and very solemnly, offered his paw.

As Martin took it, the dog looked around at the family as much as to say "This is mine. I'm staying."

Martin watched his stepfather, who was sitting quietly, obviously thinking. Martin waited, almost holding his breath, unaware that Gwyn was feeling guilty about his quick accusation of the day before. He felt he had misjudged the boy, and needed to make amends.

"Got to be sensible now," he said. "Needs a lot of thinking about. We can't just take on a dog, without working out how it might affect us all. He's been living wild; could have some disease and we don't want our dogs to catch it. Could be a very unhealthy animal. Sure to have worms, and if we keep him he needs inoculation. Your mother can drive you in to surgery when Dilys goes to work."

He knocked the top off his breakfast egg.

"Have the vet look at him. If the dog is sound, and nothing wrong with him, and you look after him, and nobody else, then yes, for a time. If anything goes wrong, he goes at once. Up to the vet, now, see?" It was the longest speech Martin had heard his stepfather make. It signalled a truce between them, for the time being.

Martin was going to keep the dog. He was quite determined.

He was only too well aware that anything might go wrong. But it wasn't going to go wrong. He would have the best German Shepherd in the country, and what was more, the dog would learn to herd sheep. He'd show Gwyn.

It was a new beginning, a plan for living, an interest for the future. No more getting up and wandering the roads, not belonging anywhere, not knowing what to do or where to go. The dog would need exercise; and teaching, and would be a companion. He put out his hand and stroked the bony back. Brown eyes gazed up at him and then the animal licked Martin's hand. It was a seal of the bond between them.

"He'll need a safe place when you're at school," Taid said. "I don't like a chained dog and he can't stay in a shed all day. I'll build him his own kennel and run. No time to watch him all day, any of us."

"Please," Martin said. It was all he could think of to say. Impassioned words were springing in his mind but he couldn't voice them. Everyone would laugh.

The family was startled by a loud knocking.

The dog gave a short bark. Anna Wyn opened the door. A tall fair haired man stood there. Brilliant blue eyes looked out of a bearded face. Beside him was a girl with fair fringed hair. Martin recognized her. She was two classes higher than he in school. He had never spoken to her.

"We came to thank your son for rescuing Tag," the man said. "I'm the little imp's father. And this is his sister, Midge."

"Come in and have a cup of coffee," Martin's mother's face lit up with a vivid smile. "How is your little boy?"

"Better than he deserves to be." The American accent sounded strange to Martin, whose ears were now tuned to Welsh voices. "They're keeping him in hospital for a couple of days. He has a broken arm, and is suffering from shock. He was lucky not to be up there still. We'd never have thought of looking for him by the wood. He's been told never to go there by himself."

"He was looking for fossils in the rocks on the wall," Midge said. "He's potty about fossils because Mike is. Tag always copies our crazes."

The dog had slipped under the table. Martin could feel its head against his ankle.

"Mike?" Dilys asked, as she prepared to leave for work. Her little mini was waiting outside the door, so that she could jump straight in and be away as soon as she had eaten. "Mike Granit. At Ty Croes. The cottage just beyond the nursery."

"Mike and Laura. I didn't know he collected fossils." Dilys was halfway to the door, always anxious about the time.

"Tag thought he saw one in one of the rocks at the bottom of the wall. The daft little coot tried to pull it out and the whole lot came tumbling down on him." His sister's voice was scornful.

"He will be O.K?" Martin asked.

"He'll be fine." The big man smiled at Martin. "Thanks to you. But we mustn't keep you. We're on our way in to town to shop. We had to say thank you. And this is for Martin." He put a parcel down on the table. " By the way, I'm Tom Pritchard. Our family came from here and settled in America two generations ago. My wife and I are trying to find our roots. You must come

66

and see us. We've a large caravan on one of the nursery fields."

They left and Martin opened his parcel. He had had no time to thank them. He would have to call in to do so and also he wanted to see Tag again. He needed to know, for his own peace of mind, that the child had recovered from his accident.

He looked at the brightly illustrated book that lay on the table in front of him.

A book of Welsh Legends, by Thomas and Margaret Pritchard.

He opened the flyleaf and read,

"Especially for Martin, who saved our small son's life. As a memento of the day he was a hero."

It was signed by both authors.

Martin stared at it. He had never met an author before. Nor had he any book he could treasure as this would be treasured.

Taid had vanished but re-appeared with a collar and leather lead. He whistled to the dog who crept out from under the table, his eyes anxious. He tried to avoid the collar, but Gwyn held him, and it was soon buckled in place.

"Need to think hard, boy," Gwyn said. "Not going to be easy at all."

Martin took the lead. The dog stared at him, and then panicked. Martin, fighting an animal that refused to move in any direction at all, realized that he had a great deal more to learn than he had imagined.

He also realized, in that moment, that the dog wasn't playing him up. It was terrified by the constriction round its neck and by being forced to move away from the safety of the kitchen. It thought it was about to be flung out into the lonely world again.

Nobody moved or spoke. Martin knew that what happened next depended on him, and on him alone. Otherwise he would lose the dog.

Chapter 7

Everyone was waiting. Martin thought hard. He knew the dog was frightened.

There was bacon rind on several of the plates. Martin collected it, and broke it into pieces. The dog, alerted by the delicious smell, watched him. Holding the rind in his hand, the boy walked towards the door. The dog, enticed by the food, walked beside him. Martin rewarded him after every few steps.

The animal jibbed at the Land Rover. Martin jumped in and held out the bacon rind.

"It won't hurt you, feller," he said. "Come on. I'm going to take care of you." For all that, the dog resisted and Gwyn lifted him in beside Martin.

The boy sat in the back, holding on to the dog.

When they reached the vet, the dog had to be dragged out of the Land Rover and into the vet. Martin began to worry. Suppose the dog never learnt confidence? Suppose he had some ghastly disease? At least he showed no sign whatever of bad temperament. He was frightened, not fierce.

Both Leah and Martin went into the room with the dog. Leah had watched her son struggle, knowing that he must cope alone if he were to keep the dog.

Martin had never seen Dilys at work before. She stood beside the examination table, wearing a white coat, a totally different person from at home. She smiled at the dog, and stroked him gently.

"No need to worry, cariad," she said. "We won't hurt you, I promise. There, then."

"So this is the milk thief?" The vet was a tall thin man. He pushed his dark hair out of his eyes before lifting the dog on to the table. He stroked him, speaking softly.

"Poor old boy. Someone's done you a dirty turn. Thrown you out into the big wide world all on your own, and you're not much more than a baby."

The crooning words were comfort. The hands on his body were re-assurance. The dog relaxed, though the worry remained in his eyes.

The vet stroked him again.

"Let's have a look at you. What a mess, to be sure. He needs good food and a bath and a lot of tender loving care. Think you're up to it, Martin? It's not going to be easy."

"He trusts me," Martin said.

"That's a start. Maybe that's all that matters."

The dog endured his examination, though still shivering. Martin held his head and stroked his neck, and prayed.

"Surprisingly healthy. A tough little animal. If you get him right he ought to make a very nice pet for you. It won't happen overnight. It'll take at least a year to begin to get any weight on him and get that coat into good condition. Cost you, too. Who's paying the bills now? Dilys says he's your dog."

Martin hadn't thought of that.

"I'll pay," he said. "Somehow. Maybe in the summer holidays I can get a job at the Sea Zoo."

He watched his mother and Dilys exchange glances. They seemed to understand one another. He wished that that understanding would spread to him. There seemed to be so many things that never included him. If he couldn't keep the dog he'd be back to nothing at all.

Vitamins. Worming powder. Flea spray. The list seemed endless.

The dog growled softly, under his breath, at the sudden prick of the needle. As soon as the syringe was empty Dilys gave him a piece of cheese.

Martin looked at the bill. To him, it seemed astronomical. It would take all his savings and more to pay it. He had never thought of a dog costing money before. But animals had to eat, and needed the vet when they were ill.

"Better insure him," the vet said. "That will help with vet bills. If he needs major surgery, the insurance firm pay."

"A broken leg could cost you over a hundred pounds," Dilys said. Martin took the leaflet and tucked it in his pocket. That would cost too.

Would his stepfather lend him the money and let him earn it back? He'd do anything to keep this dog. Even learn to like Cariad. Even sell his bike.

He needed a collar and lead; and a tag to put on the collar. How much did those cost? He couldn't keep Taid's. There were plenty of feeding bowls round the farm. There was also spare wood, but the kennel and run would cost money. Suppose Gwyn hadn't thought about the expense and changed his mind?

Martin worried all the way home, keeping the dog close beside him. The German Shepherd lay with his nose on his paws, a forlorn look in his eyes, as if unable to relax or trust life at all. Martin wondered how the animal had spent its days.

Martin had thought of calling it Rebel, but it was far from being that. Now that he had the dog he no longer felt a need to fight his family quite so hard. He was a misfit, not a rebel. He tightened his arms round the thin chest and was rewarded by a sudden swift lick round his ear.

He felt a surge of love for the dog, who had been as unwanted as he was. Now the dog was wanted, and the dog wanted Martin.

He might not belong. He could never belong, but he would try to make sure he didn't lose his dog. The stupid tricks would have to stop, or Gwyn would take the pup away.

"He needs a name, Martin," his mother said. Martin looked out of the Land Rover window at the mountains, blue shapes against a blue sky that for once hadn't a cloud in sight. He felt happier than he had done for a long time. For once he had his mother to himself. He longed to talk to her, to tell her how he felt, but the words wouldn't come.

"I think I'll call him Blue," he said, looking at the blue beyond the hills. "He came from the wild blue yonder." He didn't know where the phrase belonged, but he had heard it once and it had always stayed in his mind.

"It's a good name, Blue, isn't it?" he asked the dog, and was rewarded by a small twitch of the long tail and a lick on his hand.

They reached the farmyard, and Leah parked neatly by the wall. Martin climbed down. He expected Blue to resist, but the dog jumped out, his head in the air, sniffing. He stared at Martin, as if unable to believe his good luck. He had come back, to a place he knew.

He danced, prancing beside his new owner, joy in every movement.

He pulled eagerly towards the porch door, asking to go inside, asking to be part of the family, asking to belong.

Cariad, seeing him, vanished hastily inside her shed.

"Well now," Taid said, coming out of the kitchen doorway. "A bath for that fellow. He won't like it, but it has to be done. Can't have fleas now, can we?"

The bath was a new terror.

Blue fought, pulling and tugging until Anna Wyn came to help. Taid kept the lead on so that the dog couldn't get away. At last Blue recognized that they meant him no harm and submitted to the brushing and the rinsing with the hose.

Martin took him into the kitchen and rubbed him dry in front of the Aga. The flea powder had been mixed with shampoo.

"A lot to think of," Taid said, making coffee for them all. Anna Wyn took hers out to the barn with her, intending to drink it while she fed three lambs. Martin watched his mother make up two more bottles and follow. She seemed part of the farm now, and looked happier than she had ever looked. She also laughed more. He could help bottle feed the lambs. Would his stepfather pay him? Or pay for Blue, knowing that Martin had earned the right to keep him? He could shop for Taid. He could fetch and carry and do as he was asked without slipping off to his room, or doing every job so slowly that someone else took over.

"First things first," Taid said, apparently continuing a conversation that Martin had missed. "The dog can live free in the house now he's clean, but always on the lead outside, boy. Too easy for him to jump that fence into the sheep field."

"He's been coming for days and never touched the sheep." Martin needed to defend his new protégé.

"Don't know, do we? Might have chased them in the far fields and nobody seen him." Taid looked down at Blue, now stretched in front of the stove. Both cats had vanished through the window.

"There haven't been any damaged sheep," Martin said.

"Grant you that, boy. But a ewe in lamb can be damaged if she's chased by a dog, even if she's not hurt herself. Might lose the lamb, see?"

And that meant money. Martin couldn't help but hear Gwyn adding up his losses at times. They were black days when a ewe died, or a lamb died. Nobody could live in the farmhouse and be unaware of market prices. Gwyn had taken one group of ewes to market and brought them home unsold because the prices they were fetching were so low.

"Always something," Taid said, his mind slipping away as it often did. "Like Chernobyl now."

"Chernobyl?" Martin stared at the old man.

"You weren't here then, boy. Cloud from Russia. An atomic energy accident. Everything radioactive. We couldn't sell our sheep at all. The grass was bad, see, and it got into their bodies. The government paid, but never enough. Still some farms, years later, where the sheep can't be sold. The grass grew radioactive, see. Gave us compensation, but it's not the same." He warmed his hands on his coffee mug.

"Never know what'll happen next. Pollution in the river, and our sheep can die if they drink."

Martin knew about that. They had discussed that at school as well as the damage to the ozone layer. And mad cow disease. Gwyn was glad it wasn't a cattle farm. The salmonella scare stopped them from selling their eggs as all flocks of birds had to be tested. They only had a few hens and it wasn't worth anyone's while bothering. So no eggs for any but their own use.

"Regulations everywhere," Taid said. "People scared of their own shadows. Can't eat this. Can't do that. Not like it was when I was young. And I'm still here, aren't I?"

Martin's mother was equally impatient.

"We need to be healthy, not always running to the doctor for medicines that take away our immunity," she said, and went right on eating as she always had. They had stopped serving beef at school dinners.

"Whatever happens, the farmers suffer," Gwyn

said, when Martin told him. Martin, remembering the conversations, wondered what on earth he could do that would help; and what might be found suspect next. If there was a scare about sheep, then they would suffer too. Gwyn was scared of rustlers as well. And epidemics. Twin lamb disease could kill the tiny animals.

All of them would be affected by a drop in price; less of everything. For the first time he began to realize just what farmlife meant, and to feel as if he did have a part to play, even if he didn't fit in. Blue had given him a stake in the place, a need to help make it work.

"Nasty old world," Taid said, following some thought of his own. He shook his head as if trying to throw off his worries. "Now, that dog of yours."

My dog, Martin thought. My dog. Mine.

"How old did the vet say he was?"

"About seven months."

"Never easy taking on nobody's dog. No idea what he's learned; and most of it will be bad."

Martin hadn't thought about dogs learning. Taid's dogs were old, retired sheepdogs. That came when they were called and behaved beautifully and did as they were told. Gwyn's dogs were working dogs. He sometimes took them in for sheepdog trials and had several crooks that he had won. The collies had been trained long before he and his mother came to live on the farm.

"Lessons for both of you, boy, every day. Or

that dog won't be fit to live with. He's coming up to ten months soon. Dogs change then. They want to be off, hunting the bitches, not doing as we want. Hard work, boy."

Taid sounded as if he thought that Martin might not manage to train the dog at all.

Blue lifted his head. He stood and stretched. He yawned, then walked over to Martin and pushed his muzzle into the boy's hand.

"I'll train you better than anyone ever trained a dog before," Martin said, but he didn't say it aloud. The dog sat and looked at him, as if he knew what was in the boy's mind.

Gwyn, coming into the room, looked at all of them.

"I hope I'm doing the right thing. Against the grain to have a German Shepherd on a farm with sheep. One mistake, Martin, and the dog goes, and that's a promise."

If the dog goes, I go too, Martin thought.

"Up to you, boy," Taid said, as if guessing what was in Martin's mind. "Nobody can do it for you. You have to learn for yourself."

That, Martin knew, was not going to be easy.

Chapter 8

The homeward bus was noisy and crowded, everyone seething with excitement. Martin sat at the back, hoping he was invisible. He tried to lose himself in his own thoughts, but even they weren't pleasant.

He wished he could take his dog to school with him. Maybe he could teach Blue to bark at the boys who teased him and made his life a misery. He did not intend to learn to speak Welsh, though he was beginning to understand it, and understand too some of the remarks made about him. The other children didn't like him at all.

They thought him stuck-up and much too English. Well, he was English and what was wrong with that? Nobody could help being born, or choose the country of their birth.

Nobody at home realized that unhappiness made it difficult for him to talk to them or that he was homesick for his friends at his other school. He had been happy there. Sam Taylor could come for the summer holidays, his mother said. That was a long way off. Sam might not want to come. He would have made new friends, and maybe not want a holiday on a farm with someone he once knew.

The bus was noisy, but just for the moment everyone seemed to have forgotten him. Martin sank lower in his seat and looked out of the window at the passing hedgerows. Sheep grazed in the winter weary fields. He knew now that the grass was poor and much of Gwyn's time was spent carting hay to the fields. The sheep ran to greet him like dogs when they heard the tractor.

The journey seemed endless. The noise around him escalated. Everyone else was chattering and laughing, but the Welsh words washed over him. The other English children spoke it easily and he forgot that they weren't Welsh too.

It was a wild day, the wind whipping the tortured clouds that shrouded the mountains so that they raced across the sky. It was also Friday. Everyone was tired of the week, longing for freedom. The school was fifteen miles from home. Martin hoped he could remain unnoticed, but his luck ran out when the boy in front of him turned round and saw him.

He shouted in Welsh. The only word Martin

understood was his own name; and a yell of laughter followed it. He flushed angrily, and then the teasing began. They were three miles from the farm when the driver lost his temper. He shouted at the boys, which angered four of them to the point of making Martin's life even more unpleasant than before.

There was room for him to sit behind the driver. Perhaps he would be safer there.

It was a forlorn hope.

Wynn Davies put out a foot and tripped him, so that he fell heavily, hurting his arm against the back of the seat beside him.

He was now halfway down the bus and worse off than before.

Elwyn Jones took Martin's scarf, rolled it into a ball and threw it out of the door when the driver put down two of the girls. The man refused to stop again.

Someone pelted him with fruit drops, hitting him on the back of the neck and head. When he turned round the mocking faces were laughing, but he had no idea who was throwing the sweets.

A ruler poked him in the back and he cried out.

"Stop it. That hurt." He turned to the boy behind him, who was grinning. "Do that again and I'll thump you."

The words echoed in a sudden silence. The driver slammed on the brakes.

" Out, you. Always causing trouble, wherever

you go." Martin shivered at the sound of his voice. "Off and walk home."

Although it meant a long trudge in the drizzling rain, Martin was glad to be off the bus. The children waved and yelled as they passed. He hated them. Life was too confusing, he thought angrily, as he walked through the endless lanes.

It was the first time he had ever thought of the farm as a refuge from the world. That was because of Blue. He quickened his step. The dog would be waiting for him, would greet him eagerly and until Taid said it was lesson time, they would have fun.

He had had Blue for exactly a week, and the dog had learned little. He pulled on the lead, and often refused to come when he was called. He was afraid of most men. If a stranger came into the yard, the dog raced upstairs and hid under Martin's bed.

Martin sighed as he opened the gate and then in the next few minutes totally forgot his unhappiness, as the dog raced at him. Blue had been waiting in the kitchen doorway, watching hopefully. Somebody had tied a long line to him so that he could lie outside.

There was nothing quite like that first five minutes of ecstatic welcome, as if Martin were the most important person in the dog's world. Blue groaned with delight, barked in short frantic yelps, and danced with pleasure, his tail waving from side to side.

The farmyard was deserted. Everyone must be out with the sheep. Whenever Martin met his mother or Gwyn or Taid, or Anna Wyn, they were carrying bottles, on their way to deal with orphan lambs, or one of twins, as the mother hadn't enough milk for two.

Taid's old dog sometimes sat with a bottle in his mouth, tipped for a lamb to feed. Maybe he could teach Blue to do that. Maybe he could teach Blue to be the most wonderful dog in the world. Everyone would watch them working together and say "I wish I had a dog like that."

Daydreams didn't get you anywhere.

Where were they all?

Dilys had been talking at breakfast about the little lamb that had been adopted.

Its mother wouldn't feed it, or accept it.

Martin was suddenly curious. He left Blue tethered, and walked over the cobbles.

He crept into the barn, anxious that nobody should see him. He wasn't going to admit to any interest at all in the sheep.

The adopted lamb was as alien in the Texel herd as Martin was in his new family. It was so tiny. He stared at it, wondering about it. It was black-legged, a shaggy little animal with an appealing black face, totally unlike its shaggy grey foster mother. It trotted trustingly up to him, and sucked furiously at his finger. It had already been bottle fed and associated people with milk as well as the big ewe.

She glared at Martin as if he were about to hurt her baby. So she had accepted it after all.

The little creature began to suck.

"There now," said Taid's voice behind Martin. "You've done what we couldn't do. That's the first time she's shown any real interest in it." Martin stared at him.

"What did I do?"

"She doesn't know you as well as she does us. Probably doesn't know you at all. You came too near the baby, and roused her protective instinct. I was going to bring a dog in; that often works. The ewe guards the baby and then forgets it isn't hers."

Martin felt an unexpected glow of satisfaction. He had done something useful at last. Maybe they'd realize he wasn't always a nuisance.

Taid walked across the barn to feed yet another lamb. Martin went back to Blue, who was lying with his nose on his paws, staring forlornly at nothing. The dog leaped up, licking at the boy's face. Martin crouched, his arms round the animal. Taid had began to ease his misery. Now, for the moment, the cure was complete.

Martin felt happier than he had for months.

Chapter 9

He was free from school, free from teasing, and the whole weekend lay ahead.

Two glorious days to share with Blue.

Early on Saturday morning Martin leashed his dog, and walked up the hill. Blue pulled for the first half mile. Martin wished he knew how to stop that. Then the dog settled. He showed no sign of wanting to chase the sheep, although Martin had taken a path through the fields.

"You can walk with him through the fields. Keep him on the lead. Never let him off," Gwyn said.

Martin suddenly realized that that was trust too. There was a bounce in his step, and a joy in being out with the dog. He couldn't have had a dog in their flat in Chester. There were some advantages to living on the farm.

It was a dry day in late March, with Spring very definitely in the air. Martin sat on a rocky outcrop and looked down at the farm. His mother's garden was glowing with daffodils, planted in the lawn in great drifts.

It had been a wilderness when she'd started on it. But you'd never know that to look at it now.

Martin leaned against the rock and tried to order his thoughts.

In some ways he felt more alone than ever. No one intended to help him look after the dog, though Taid promised to help train him. A dog, Martin discovered, made a great deal of difference to his life. He no longer had so much free time. He spent his days in a very different way.

Until Taid built his kennel and run, Blue had to be locked in one of the sheds when Martin was at school. He had to be trained every day. He had to be fed. He had to be groomed. Taid let the boy borrow the brush he used on his own dogs. Blue ought to have one of his own.

There was the shed to clean out: damp straw removed and fresh put in, the floor swept.

"Don't want your dog crippled with arthritis before he's four years old," Taid said.

Blue had to have his breakfast before Martin went off to school. The bowl had to be washed and dried and put away, and water put down to last the day. The dog also had to have a walk. Leah bought her son an alarm clock that was set every day to half-past six.

"Your dog, boy," Gwyn said. "Your responsibility."

"Be a challenge," Taid said. "Good for all of us, challenges. Make us grow up."

He saw Martin's expression and laughed.

"Even at my age, boy. Or you just sit around waiting for nothing with nothing to get up for, see? I like having plenty to do, though can't do as much now as I did."

Taid gave Martin lessons with his dog. Though it didn't feel like training at all.

The old man stitched the clip from a worn out dog lead on to a thirty foot length of soft rope. Martin had it with him now. It would be a good idea to give the dog an extra lesson. It wasn't always easy to remember what he had been taught.

He would give the dog a "come" lesson. It was the first time he had thought of doing that while he was out for a walk.

Martin put the long line on the dog's collar. Blue looked at him. He knew what that meant, and it didn't always mean fun.

Martin walked a little distance, letting the dog run out on the line.

"Blue, come."

Maybe today the lesson would work. Martin

had put bacon rind in his pocket. He broke it into pieces, and held a piece out.

Blue didn't always want to come. Yesterday's lesson had been a bad one, and Martin ended it feeling as if the dog would never learn.

There were smells on the ground, from sheep; from rabbits and sometimes from the fox. Blue tried to follow them, eager to chase, and Martin discovered it took all his strength to stop himself being pulled over.

"Tell him he's a good dog when he comes to you, boy," Taid said, over and over. "Only way he knows he's doing right. Sound as if you mean it."

Often Martin didn't mean it. He called and Blue ignored him. It was easy to feel defeated by the dog. Easy to feel irritated.

"Never lose your temper with him, boy," Taid said. "Never have a good dog if you lose his trust."

Martin thought of all the things he needed to remember.

Sometimes when he tugged on the line the dog came, then stopped halfway to seek out an even more interesting smell than that he had just left.

"All his brains in his nose, boy," Taid said. "Look at the grass; there's been pheasants there, and he knows it. See the marks in the grass where they walked."

There was so much to think about, but Martin was beginning to understand what triggered his dog to misbehave. The boy was tongue tied and shy with most people. He found it difficult to praise Blue when Taid was there. He felt silly.

That morning, his spirits high, Martin called his dog with so much enthusiasm that Blue ran to him excitedly. Martin gave him a piece of bacon rind.

At the end of ten minutes the dog was behaving as if he had been trained for weeks. Martin, jubilant, and encouraged by his dog's behaviour, climbed the footpath stile on to the road that led to the garden centre.

He hesitated at the gate and then went in. A merry little woman with a laughing face put down the box of plants she was carrying and came towards him.

"You'll be Martin. I've seen you when I've passed Bryn Gwynt. Tag's rescuer. Have you come to see him? He's been hoping you'd call. Go through the gate at the bottom of the nursery and cross the first field. Their caravan is just beyond the hedge."

She picked up the box of plants and strode off. Martin, holding Blue close against him lest his tail broke one of the many plants that lined the path, went through the little wicket gate and out into the field.

A path led across the middle to another gate. Beyond it he heard voices.

The kissing gate led along a crazy paving path

to a corner shielded by large shrubs. He turned it to face the largest caravan he had ever seen. It was made from two enormous vans, and there was a garden around it, just as there was round a suburban house. Daffodils sprang out of huge tufts of flowering heather and later there would be roses on the bare bushes.

The door was flung open and a tall girl exploded out of it, shouting. The curls that tumbled from her head bounced on her shoulders, and blew in the wind. She stared at Martin.

"Hey. That's some dog. You must be Martin. Want to see Tag? He's being impossible. He can't do anything much with his arm in plaster and he's cross as a fox shut in a cage. Come on in."

Martin followed her into an enormous sitting room, with huge windows that framed the mountains.

"Mom, this is Martin who saved Tag. Though I don't know why he bothered. Little beast."

"I'm not."

Tag's mother was painting. The line of mountains gleamed in the sun of a different day, shining at Martin from the easel. He stared at it, fascinated. It must be wonderful to paint like that. She was very like Tag, small and blonde and stocky with brilliant blue eyes that laughed at Martin.

"Neither of them is fit to live with today. Come into our madhouse. Tag doesn't know what to

90

do with himself as it's his right arm that's out of action."

"I can still hit Midge with it, and I will if she doesn't stop teasing me," Tag's eyes glittered with anger. Any moment now and he'd pounce like a cat, Martin thought.

Blue was pressed against Martin's leg. He could feel the dog shivering.

"Hey, is that your dog?" Tag moved fast towards them. Blue pulled his lead out of Martin's hand, leaped through the door and raced down the hill towards the sheep field.

Martin pelted after him, calling.

Gwyn's words sounded relentlessly in his brain.

"Just one mistake, boy, and he goes."

"I'll get him," Midge said, charging after Martin.

"No. He's scared. He doesn't know you. Please don't go after him. Leave it to me."

Midge didn't listen. She tore after Blue. The faster she ran, the faster the dog ran.

Taid's words flashed into Martin's brain.

"Never run after your dog. Run away and he'll follow. They hate being alone."

If only it worked. He turned and began to run back the way they had come, calling. He could never catch the dog. Blue was out of his mind with terror, among strangers who were chasing him as he must have been chased before.

"Blue, Blue boy. Here then," he called, his voice desperate.

Behind him, Midge pelted on, chasing the dog further and further away from him.

Martin's head ached with misery.

The dog would run for ever and never come back.

Chapter 10

Martin dared not look back. He was certain that Blue would jump into the fleeing sheep. They saw the dog racing towards them, and panicked, running in a milling mob, bleating at the tops of their voices.

Martin had never seen sheep so frightened. He had visions of his dog worrying and mauling them. Of Gwyn saying the dog must be put to sleep.

If only Midge had listened. She was terrifying the dog even more, and there was no way he would ever take any notice of Martin's calls.

The dog was in a blind panic.

Maybe he would be too frightened to touch the sheep and just run, and run, and run. Martin would never catch up with him. Would never see him again. The dog would never find his way back to Bryn Gwynt. His tormented life would start all over again.

It had already started.

Martin reached the hedge. It was useless. Taid's advice hadn't worked. Blue was still pelting towards the sheepfield. Martin was sure the dog could jump the fence. Midge was still racing on, sure she could catch up with the animal.

"Midge, stand still." There was authority in the quiet voice. Martin turned his head. It was Tom Pritchard, Tag's father. He was walking unhurriedly across the field on a path that would intercept the dog.

Midge stopped running.

Blue had not noticed the newcomer. He was intent on escape. Tom Pritchard moved forward, and as the dog flew past him, he stepped on the trailing lead. Blue stopped, shocked by the sudden braking.

Martin swallowed the lump in his throat and tore across the grass. He knelt beside his dog, holding the panting body, feeling the shake of fear.

"Oh, Blue, Blue," he said.

The dog pressed against him, desperate.

Tom Pritchard crouched beside them.

"There, there, fella." It was a low croon, almost under his breath. "It's OK. You're safe now. Quite safe. What made him bolt?" His hands caressed the dog's back. "This is the dog that's been running wild round the village, isn't it?"

Everyone in the village seemed to know everything about everyone else, Martin thought.

He nodded.

"He's scared of people. Tag moved too fast. He had his hand out to stroke, but Blue thought he was going to hit him." Martin wondered how he knew, but he was sure he was right. He had spent so much time with the dog that he could guess some of his reactions.

"He's every reason to be scared of people. He's been chivvied and shouted at. Had stones thrown at him. Ianto Ty Newydd shot at him. The dog was in his sheepfield. Luckily he missed."

Martin hugged Blue. The dog had suffered from cruel people just as he had.

"Thank you for stopping him."

"My pleasure. I like dogs. It'll take a long time for him to forget what's happened to him. He may never forget."

Blue looked up at the big man. The gentle hands re-assured him. He waved his tail, a mere hint of a wave, but an acknowledgement.

"If I were you I'd take him home and let him lie quietly in his bed. When he's feeling more secure we'll give young Tag a lesson on how to approach Blue without scaring him silly. "

Martin picked up the lead. Tom Pritchard took it from him.

"I'll come with you. He's a strong dog and if

we meet something else that frightens him, you might not be able to hold him."

Had anyone else said that Martin would have been angry. Instead, he felt grateful. Blue, when fear mastered him, was apt to behave like a panicking horse.

"I used to have a German Shepherd, when we were in the States," Tom said. "Trained him to track and search, just like a police dog. I miss him."

He grinned at Martin, his dark eyes laughing. "Want to try? Then when that imp of mine loses himself, as he does twice a week and three times on Sundays, we can ask Blue to find him."

Martin didn't know how to express his excitement. If only this man were his stepfather instead of Gwyn, who was always so busy and never had time to listen. Never wanted to listen.

"Just let him settle for a few minutes," Tom said. Blue was lying at his feet, exhausted by his fear and his wild race to nowhere.

Below them, the farm was a doll's house, where tiny animals stood in the fields, as if a giant child had placed them there, playing its own games.

They strolled down the hill. Martin was busy with his own thoughts. Tag's father seemed to have no desire to speak, but just his presence was comforting.

They walked into the yard just as a small white van drove up and parked beyond them.

Dilys climbed out.

"I need hands. I've a major problem." She was too concerned to question the newcomer, or even ask if he were prepared to help. Martin stared at her as if seeing her for the first time. A dark haired slender girl, always impatient except with animals.

From inside the van came the most incredible squealing.

Anna Wyn erupted from the kitchen, a bottle in her hand.

"What in the world have you brought us now?"

"A present for the sanctuary. A Vietnamese Pot Bellied pig. She's about to farrow, and her owner's decided she can't cope with dozens of little pigs everywhere. She can go in the old sty."

Anna Wyn opened the van door and was greeted by a frenzied grunting. Martin looked at the largest pig he had ever seen, her gigantic belly spread out around her on the ground.

"We'll never get her out," Anna Wyn said.

"No choice. The owner wants the van back and anyway, she can't have her babies there. They're due any minute. It's all hands on the job."

"It looks some job." Tom Pritchard's voice held laughter. "Count me in. I'm no pigman, but I can always learn. I've useful hands and I can stop a dog at two paces."

He winked at Martin.

"Put Blue out of the way. That noise is enough to make him run from here to Dallas. All we

97

need to panic him for good is for Madam here to explode and run us down. She looks big enough to crush us."

Martin shut Blue in his shed. He returned to the yard to find the noises from the van had increased to a crescendo. Tom Pritchard crouched at the back of the van, making soothing noises that hadn't a chance of being heard.

Inappropriately, he appeared to be singing "Coming through the rye," and both Dilys and Anna Wyn had dissolved into laughter.

He straightened himself up.

"I once travelled round the Scottish islands with an old farmer and a bull going to market," he said. He grinned, remembering. "The beast was massive. He was lashed into a crate. The old man was fat, his clothes bursting off him and he wore a greasy pork pie hat. He sang hymns non stop to keep the animal from panicking."

"Why?" Martin asked.

"It soothes them. I once sat on a lonely beach playing my recorder, as nobody liked me practising at home. The seals came to listen."

He laughed again.

"Most people think I'm quite mad, but I have had a lot to do with frightened animals. I once worked for a man who rescued injured birds and beasts."

"Then you can help us," Dilys said, without bothering to find out whether Tom wanted to or not. "We always need extra help."

98

Tom walked across the yard and looked at the pigsty.

"You can't put her in there. It's too dirty. Those piglets will end up sick."

Dilys, standing behind him, sighed.

"It's years since we had a pig."

"What about the whelping kennel we had ready for the brood bitch we never got?" Anna Wyn asked. She had made it hopefully, whitewashed the walls, and built a run. Taid had suggested it as a home for Blue, but Anna Wyn was still determined to have her way. One day.

She wanted to breed Great Danes, and had picked out her foundation stock, only to have her father say that they hadn't nearly enough time to add pups to their other commitments. That was before Leah came. Anna Wyn hoped desperately that she would soon have an ally.

"She'll do there for a week or two; till the sty's ready," Dilys said. "The building's strong; it's stone." There were so many outbuildings round the farm that Martin had never explored them all. He had not been interested before.

Dilys backed the van across the yard.

"Has she a name?" Anna Wyn asked, as they re-opened the back doors.

"Harriet," Dilys said, and the others laughed.

"People do give animals the oddest names," Tom said.

"What would you call her?" Dilys's voice was defensive.

"Off hand, I don't know. After the goddess of fertility, I should think. Who was she? Hera? Ceres? I'd have to look it up. Welsh legends are my chief interest, not Roman or Greek."

The door to the kennel was wide open and so were the doors of the van. Tom helped Dilys manoeuvre a heavy old door to act as a ramp. The back of the van was high off the ground.

Harriet's worried face said plainly that if anyone expected to walk a pig of her size and condition down that they could think again. Her small hooves were set like rocks, but she had stopped squealing and was now grunting continuously.

"She's telling us we're daft, and I'm not at all sure she's not right." Tom scratched his ear. "How on earth did you get her in there?"

"No problem. She's used to that. It belongs to her owner and she's been in it several times, to the vet and so on."

Martin wondered what so on meant with a pig. Walks in the woods? Swimming in the sea? He was beginning to discover, from listening to Dilys, that animal owners often did the oddest things.

"She doesn't like it here," Martin said. "It isn't home."

Tom looked at him, saying nothing. He understands, Martin thought. Realization flashed across his mind. The Pritchards were not only in a strange country, but in a different continent, thousands of miles away from their own birth-place.

Harriet put a hoof on the ramp, and then withdrew to the back of the van, standing knee deep in shavings.

"Now what do we do?" Dilys held out a carrot. Harriet decided she was blind. "She's far to big to drag. She can't be carried. You can't put a lead round her neck; it wouldn't stay on. And she hasn't a ring through her nose."

She held out the carrot again. This time Harriet put both front hooves on the ramp, and slid. She retreated fast to safety.

"She'll hurt herself." Dilys sounded forlorn.

"More likely to hurt us," Tom said. "She might make up her mind to charge down that ramp and across the yard, trying to escape."

"She's too big to move fast," Anna Wyn said.

"She might surprise us all."

Martin went indoors. Blue worked for bacon rind, so why not the pig? But tiny titbits wouldn't work with something that size. He poured a whole packet of cereal into the washing-up bowl and added milk.

"Good idea," Tom said, when Martin returned.

"Thought you'd done a runner," said Anna Wyn.

Harriet stretched out her thick neck and sniffed noisily. She wanted the food, but fear of sliding prevented her from moving. She withdrew, snorting, to safety.

Martin looked at her, standing there knee deep in shavings. The girls watched him, not knowing what had come over him. Not knowing how much he needed to win approval from Tom Pritchard.

Harriet was scared. She felt ill at ease and unhappy and she knew she was only safe in the van. Martin picked up the coal shovel from its place by the back door and climbed into the van. He pushed the shavings from around the pig, until she was standing on bare metal and the ramp was heavily covered.

"Good thinking, son," Tom Pritchard said, and Martin felt a small inward glow of pleasure.

The van floor was unpleasant to stand on without the layer of shavings. Harriet moved slowly towards the ramp and then, more purpose-fully, as the shavings were familiar and smelled of her, she walked down it. Confidence restored, she charged the last few steps, pushing Anna Wyn out of the way. Martin held the bowl towards her, and the desire for food blotted out all other feelings.

Martin backed into her new home and put the bowl down in the far corner. Dilys had spread shavings on the floor, and Tom took a shovelfull from the van ramp and threw those in after as she buried her nose in the washing-up bowl. He shut the door.

"Those shavngs smell of her now," he said. "That ought to help her settle." He closed the gate of the large compound.

"Time I was off. They'll be wondering where I

am. See you, Martin. Remember we're going to teach Blue."

Martin watched him stride up the hill. He envied Midge and Tag, They had a real father, not a man who left them and went to the other side of the world. Nor a stepfather who seemed totally alien and robbed them of their mother's company.

Gwyn and Leah had been visiting. By the time they returned Harriet was settled. Gwyn went out to look at her. Martin slipped away. He had no desire that anyone should remember that he had actually been helpful. He'd have no time to himself at all if they thought they could count on him every time they needed an extra pair of hands.

Later that evening he looked through the little window at the pig. She was sound asleep, her enormous body stretched out on the straw. Her big face looked peaceful now and he realized that even a pig could have a worried expression in her eyes. She had definitely been afraid, there in the van. He knew that fear. Fear of a new experience, of a different home, of strangers all around you.

Martin walked over to Blue's shed and released him. The dog was allowed in the kitchen in the evenings and he slept indoors. Leah said he would keep them safe from burglars, which he couldn't do in a kennel.

The kitchen was bright and welcoming. The

family seated at the table suddenly comforting. Gwyn looked at him, one eyebrow angled. Taid's bright eyes bored into Martin's soul.

Blue stretched out on the rug in front of the Aga. Sweep leapt to the top of the dresser, her tail lashing. Sooty sat smugly on Anna Wyn's lap, knowing the dog would not chase her while she was there.

"It's freezing out there," Martin said, anxious to take some part.

"I'll need all the hot water bottles there are," Dilys said. "I can't leave Harriet alone tonight. She can hardly have piglets in the warm kitchen. It's going to be cold in her sty."

Martin bit into his meat pie. The pig had looked as if she would sleep through the night, he thought. There would be no birth yet.

He reached out his hand for the pickle jar, and as he did so the silence outside was rent with agonized squeals.

Everyone ran, all thought of food forgotten.

Chapter 11

Everyone looked in disbelief. The noise came from a newborn piglet, whose brother appeared to be trying to eat him.

Harriet lay with two other little pigs already sucking from her. As she grunted, yet another baby appeared, standing as soon as it was born, and running round its mother to stare in astonishment at her face. Then it began to hunt for food.

Martin had never realized that little pigs were born with open eyes, and able to run almost as soon as they breathed. Dilys shifted the piglet's mouth from his brother's ear and put both of them to suck.

"What a noise," Leah said. "I'd never thought anything so tiny could squeal so loudly."

"You'd squeal if I tried to eat your ear," Anna

Wyn said. "Just wait till we wean them and feeding time comes near. You can hear them for miles. Aren't they gorgeous? Isn't she clever?"

Harriet grunted loudly, as another piglet appeared from under her tail.

"I don't think this breed have big litters," Anna Wyn said.

"No use to anyone." Gwyn was smiling as he said it. He always liked baby animals on the farm, whether lambs or pups or kittens or little chicks.

"They'll be a star attraction when we open the sanctuary as a childrens' zoo," Dilys said.

"Can't call it a Zoo. We'll need another name. And there's lots to do before we can begin. We'll never be ready for Easter." Leah sounded dispirited.

"Better be," Dilys said. "I've been telling all our clients about it. And about our wonderful cream teas."

"Who'll be doing those, then?" Taid asked.

"Leah and Anna Wyn."

Martin didn't wait to hear the rest of the conversation. Everyone was watching Harriet, as if she were the only thing that mattered in the world. A stupid pig having little pigs. Sows did that all the time. What was so wonderful about this one?

He went back to the kitchen, where Blue stood to greet him, his body half crouched, his ears flat, his tail low. The dog had known too much misery in his short life to trust any human yet.

106

He was saying, in the only way he knew, that he was a good dog, and didn't intend to challenge anyone.

Martin knelt and put his arms round the dog. Blue relaxed, sensing misery, and licked the boy's face.

"You and me against the world," Martin said. "One day, you'll be the most fantastic dog."

One day seemed a long time coming. The daily lessons went on. Blue learned to come as soon as Martin called him, and was rewarded with a tiny slivers of liver, which Taid baked hard in the oven and then cut into pieces no bigger than his little finger nail.

"Always tempts a dog," he said. "Later, when they've learned, you don't need to give them food. But it's the quickest way to teach any frightened, nervous, or baby animal."

"Who taught you to train dogs?" Martin asked one morning. "Wyn Davies, at school, says you never use titbits. He says its daft. The dog will only work for food, not for you."

"My own Taid. And experience. A dog has to learn to love you and trust you before he works for your love. Why should he work for love when he doesn't know you? That way he works out of fear of you hurting him if he doesn't do right."

The old man was often fierce when it came to the ways to train animals.

"That trust has to be earned; if you feed him, that's nature; his mother fed him and he loved her

107

because of it. Blue has a long way to go. Boys at school don't know everything."

When Blue's lessons went well they spent longer teaching him. When they went badly they made sure that Blue did at least one thing right before they finished, and then played with the dog. He loved jumping and Taid made him several little hurdles out of two large plant pots, with a slender wooden lathe across them.

"Play is as important as lessons," Taid said. "It teaches him to enjoy being with us; to trust us; and to get to know us. It will also become a bigger reward than his food, one day. When then happens, you'll know we've begun to make real progress."

Sometimes at weekends Martin went up to the caravan to talk to Tag. His real reason was the hope that Tom Pritchard might be there. The big man was so easy to talk to, was interested in everyone, and made an immense fuss of Blue.

By the start of the Easter holidays the little sanctuary was ready to open. Taid had made enclosures for the animals, working every day. There was a sandpit and a climbing frame, and local children had donated outgrown toys. Taid built a Wendy house, and furnished it with mushroom stools, brightly painted in scarlet and white, and little tables.

Anna Wyn made curtains for the windows, from material patterned with rabbits, and there were colouring books and crayons and brightly coloured picture books. There was also an easel on which were sheets of blank paper, with paints beside it.

"We'll write to all the nursery schools," Anna Wyn said. "If they bring parties of children round we'll soon get known."

The villagers, Martin discovered, were always ready to help if possible. Soon there was a pen of rabbits, donated by families who had wondered what to do with them as the children grew up. Dilys arrived one afternoon driving a strange horse box, from which she unloaded a Shetland pony, heavily in foal.

Blue had to be taken round the sanctuary on his lead, morning after morning, and taught to ignore the animals. He was fascinated by the rabbits, and at first tried to catch the fantail pigeons and the doves that flew in and out of the little nesting places. It seemed to be an endless process as every time a new creature came to the sanctuary, Blue wanted to know all about it.

"Safer than keeping him away from them. If he gets used to them he'll learn they aren't to be chased or harmed," Taid said.

That was easier said than done as Blue became excited and wanted to chase and Martin had to learn how to keep him very still, sitting beside a pen, watching its inmates run around. It wasn't easy, but slowly, Martin was becoming interested.

The dog meant more to him than any other living creature. Blue knew he belonged to Martin.

He was forlorn when shut in the kennel and run that Taid had made. He was always waiting, looking for the school bus, eager to greet his master, eager to be released, eager for their time together.

"I'll never get Blue steady," Martin said one Saturday afternoon, sitting on the floor in the Pritchards' caravan. Anna Wyn had been given two chipmunks the day before. They were lively little squirrel-like animals with striped tails. They leaped around the cage, triggering Blue to frenzy so that he barked at them and tried to paw the wire. In the end Taid had taken the dog and made him stay in front of them. He wouldn't sit still for Martin.

"You'll never do anything," Midge said. "You give up all the time. What's the matter with you? It's easy to teach a dog."

"She's never done it." Tag had transferred his allegiance from his sister to Martin, and, whenever he could, tagged after his new friend at the weekends.

"You've never done it either," said Midge. "You're too small and too daft."

"That's enough." Martin hadn't seen the childrens' father arrive. "What's all the fuss about?"

Tag, his face bright red, was holding a cushion, about to hurl it at his sister.

"Midge says its easy to train a dog and Martin's stupid."

"That's not what I said."

"Never mind what anyone said. Martin, bring Blue and come outside with me. And you two, just get on with your jobs. You both promised your mother you'd tidy your rooms. Tag's seems to have had burglars who have thrown everything on to the floor, and nobody can get inside yours, Midge. So jump to it, now."

Martin was glad to leave the caravan. Midge, now she knew him well, was increasingly bossy, and very far from complimentary. She always made him feel stupid, as if her brain ran ahead of his and he had to think hard to catch up. Sometimes he never did catch up and couldn't understand her at all.

"That dog loves using his nose," Tom Pritchard said. "Have you noticed how, whenever he's outside, he keeps it down on the ground? He's just taken us over the path that Tag walked about an hour ago. Look, there's the ball he lost. Blue's found it."

The dog was nosing in a clump of long grass. A large solid red ball suddenly appeared and rolled. Blue sat and watched it, his eyes bright.

"Time to start teaching him to search and track," Tom said. "That's what police dogs do. They have to hunt for clues after a crime. Maybe a burglar drops something he's just stolen, or a tool he used to break in. The dog finds it, and is taught to lie still beside it, so that he doesn't rub out the fingerprints by picking it up in his mouth."

"Can we teach Blue? How do you teach him?"

"Easy," Tom said "And it's great fun." He tossed the ball to Blue, who caught it on his nose, and knocked it a few yards. He pounced on it and picked it up.

"He knows about balls already," Tom said. "Someone's played with him in the past. I wonder who owned him and what happened to him before you found him?"

"He found me," Martin said. He felt a sudden thrill of interest. If he could teach this dog to search and track like a police dog, maybe Gwyn would take some notice of him. He might even approve of him. Maybe the girls would be impressed. Maybe his mother would find time for him again. Maybe after all there was something he could do. Everyone at home and at school seemed to spend their time telling him he was useless.

"I never do anything right," he said now, despairingly. If only he had a father like Tom. Midge and Tag didn't know how lucky they were. "Everything I do goes wrong and something awful happens and they think I do it on purpose."

"It's never easy, moving from one place to another. It's a bit like being born all over again and not knowing anything. You have to learn it. The towns are very different to the country and you can make so many mistakes without thinking. Like leaving gates open and letting all the cows or sheep out. Both Midge and Tag did that at first. They were most unpopular until they learned.

Why doesn't anyone at the farm tell me? Martin wondered. I'm supposed to know, or guess, and how can I if nobody ever says anything?

"How do we teach Blue?" Martin asked. He didn't want to think about all the mistakes he'd made, both intentional and by mistake.

"It'll take a long time. He won't learn overnight. You didn't learn to read in a day, did you? It will take as long for Blue to understand what we want. We can't tell him. We have to show him. Let's go up the hill and onto the moorland."

The path led through a large bare field with grass too sparse for the sheep. Gwyn moved them every two weeks, so that no field was too foul. They climbed over a stile, on to the high moor. Beyond was dead bracken and heather, the new growth just beginning. Trees, fuzzy with swelling buds, clothed the horizon and hid the Straits. The distant church spire stood high above the woods.

"Throw the ball twice for Blue to fetch," Tom said.

This was a different dog. A happy eager dog, his tail waving. This was fun, a remembered game from some long ago time when the dog had been a pup. His playfulness infected Martin, who felt suddenly light-hearted and happier than he could remember being for a long time.

"Take it from him. Say "Give", and mind you dont hurt his mouth. Those lips are tender."

Blue was reluctant to give Martin the ball. Tom

113

laughed, and held out his hand. The dog knew that the man would take it, however hard he held on. He released it.

"You always have to win, with a dog," Tom said. "Otherwise he becomes Boss, and that can lead to bites. Don't ever run away from him with the ball. He'll chase after it and try to snatch it and bite by accident. He won't mean it but it'll still hurt."

Think for him. He can't. Tom's words repeated themselves in Martin's brain. He was learning a new way to look at the world, but as yet he didn't realize what he was learning.

" People don't understand animals these days," Tom said. "They expect them to behave far better than humans and then are shocked when they behave the way nature intended. If children were taught how to behave when dogs are near, none of them would ever be bitten. And pigs would grow on trees," he added, laughing. "Give me his lead."

Martin handed over the lead, wondering if Blue would object. He did not always like other people taking him away from his master. The dog sat at Tom's feet, looking up at him, and Martin felt a small stab of jealousy. Blue never looked at him quite in that way. Nor did he obey so easily.

"Take the ball and throw it up and down, playing with it," Tom said. "Take it to the edge of the moor and hide it. Then we'll see if he can find it."

Behind him, as he threw the ball, Martin heard an eager bark. It was the first time the dog had barked. Blue wanted that ball and wanted it badly.

"He's an easy dog to teach and he's going to be great fun, Martin. We'll do it together and maybe young Tag'll join in. It will do him good."

Martin didn't want to share his dog, above all he didn't want to share him with Tag who could be a nuisance, but he did want to teach Blue. He couldn't do it alone. He didn't know how and he had to learn. He would rather Tom Pritchard taught him than Taid. Taid was part of his mother's new family, even though he did make time for Martin.

He would train his dog and surprise everyone.

"The ball's to share with Blue as a special treat. If he has it all the time it would be like you having a birthday every day; no fun at all. One a year, wow, that's great. A birthday every day would soon become a bore. Nothing to hope for."

A birthday every day sounded great. Or did it? Tom stroked the dog's head gently. Blue looked up at him, trust in his eyes.

"For Blue, once or twice a day; or he'll get tired of it. Then we won't get him wanting to learn how to find it in a very difficult place."

This time Martin walked into the long grass, and hid the ball some distance from the path.

"Look for a landmark near it," Tom called.

"That big clump of dead heather; is there anything else close?"

"A bit of rock," Martin said.

"It's easy to forget where you put it and if you don't take the dog near enough, he can't find it either. Later, when Blue's under control he can run free; but not yet. He's a lot to learn."

The dog nosed his way along the path, following Martin's footsteps. He stopped and sniffed in a circle at the edge of the rough ground and then, as if he had been glued to the earth, he turned off the path, along the trail, and picked up the ball.

Martin was so impressed that his praise came more quickly than Tom's as he stroked and patted his dog and told him how great he was and then threw the ball for Blue to catch.

"He tracked that. He found it by following your footsteps. He's a terrific dog," Tom said. "We'll go a long way with him, Martin. There's so much we can teach him, and this breed needs to learn or they get wicked because they've nothing to make them use their brains. Like boys. Game to try?"

Tom needed no reply as Martin looked up at him, excitement lighting his eager face.

Chapter 12

School was a penance. Martin dreaded the mornings, dreaded the sight of the bus, dreaded the hours in the playground. All the other boys seemed to have friends, but he had none. He tried his hardest to become invisible but it wasn't easy. Two of his tormentors seemed to spend all their time looking for him, or devising new ways of making his life a misery.

They scrawled in his school books, so that he was blamed. They hid the equipment he needed for his next lessons. They put beetles and snails in his desk and told the teacher he was collecting them.

He had no idea how to fight back, and it seemed little use complaining to anyone. Nobody ever believed him. If it hadn't been for Blue and his weekends with the Pritchards, he would have run away.

The early morning walks were his main delight. Nobody else was about. The world was his and his alone. He took a red ball with him, and hid it for Blue to find. The dog couldn't wait for the game. He watched with eager eyes, his whole body alight with excitement, his tail waving, his legs dancing.

It was all Martin could do to hold the line when he gave Blue the command "Find". He never let Blue run free. There might be sheep loose in the lanes, and Blue could jump walls.

The line gave him a range of sixty feet. Blue could still have a great deal of fun and exercise. And Martin could relax, knowing the dog couldn't get free and chase or kill. He could reel him in, and was learning to do that fast.

He longed for each weekend, so that he could show Tom Pritchard how the dog had progressed.

He was unaware that he was becoming much more sensitive to the animals and their feelings. Even to Cariad. He too now thought that her mischief was often funny.

He tried, at night, when he couldn't sleep, to imagine how Blue had felt, running wild, cold, wet, alone, and half starving. He knew that Blue was scared of pain, and was terrified of sticks.

One morning he discovered another of Blue's fears.

Martin carried the post in, and handed it to

Gwyn. It contained a rolled up newspaper. The dog was in the kitchen. Blue took one appalled look at the package and fled under the table.

" Dogs never lie. You can always tell what's happened to them. Somebody used that to try and teach him, or to punish him," Gwyn said. "Not a way I like, boy. It's old fashioned advice, like giving naughty children bread and water and a night locked in a dark cupboard. Only a lunatic would do that now. Yet the Victorians thought it the proper way to deal with a child that had done wrong."

Martin stared at his stepfather, appalled. Surely nobody had ever done that? He couldn't imagine anything more terrifying, except perhaps being soundly beaten. Gwyn was still speaking.

" Unless you can get the dog on your side it's no use trying. Kindness always works."

Martin, on his knees trying to coax Blue out, couldn't think of anything to say. He nodded.

"Give him my breakfast bacon, boy," Gwyn cut the crisp rasher into small pieces. "That might persuade him we don't mean any harm. I'll not open the post till you've taken him outside."

Even with the offer of crisp grilled bacon, Blue was reluctant to face the open space. He felt safe under the table. At last he followed Martin out of the room, but raced into his pen, and sat at the back of it, refusing to come out again.

Martin wondered what memory had been triggered by the newspaper. There was so much he didn't know about this dog. He glanced at his watch.

He was late. He rushed indoors to collect his books. He would have to run, down the lane and along the road, or the school bus would be gone. Martin had enough black marks to his name already.

He passed Anna Wyn carrying a small box.

"Bats," she said, looking at Martin. He stared back, wondering why she had to be hurtful, but there was no time to stop.

He jumped the gate and tore down the lane, resentment blotting out every other feeling.

It was the last day of term. A whole fortnight lay ahead, without the need to go to school. Two weeks, with every day to spend with Blue. No tormenting from other boys. No mocking smiles from the girls who seemed to enjoy his discomfort.

Time to heal a little, time to hope a little, and time to pray that next term his two chief enemies would have forgotten him, would be more used to him, and would not set him up as a deliberate target.

The other children were also excited at the thought of end of term. Silliness pervaded the playground, but for once they didn't play tricks on him, or say things that hurt. They confined themselves to speaking in Welsh, and refusing to understand anything Martin said. He felt more alone than ever.

The next morning was bright and sunny, with a hint of frost in the air. Easter was late. It was already mid April, but it was still cold.

Tom Pritchard was writing at his desk when Martin called. He put down his pen at once, and came outside to watch Blue hunt for his ball.

"He's doing well," Tom said. "No school for two weeks, so you can come up here every day for an hour or so. That's the virtue of being a freelance."

"What's a freelance?" Martin asked.

"Someone who works for himself and chooses when to work. I can sleep all day and work all night if I feel like it," Tom laughed, "which I don't. But I can take an hour off when I choose, and work in the evening. It'll be fun to watch Blue progress."

"I don't want to go back to school, ever." Martin sat on the doorstep. He put his arms round the dog.

"Giving you a hard time?" Tom asked. "They did that to Midge at first. She found out how to fit in."

"How?"

"Mainly by learning Welsh. She speaks it as if she'd lived here all her life now. She can also answer back, and she knows how to make people laugh so that they forget to tease her. Her mother and I are learning it too, and Tag is a little mimic; he can speak it as well as Midge.

It's easier to learn languages when you're very young."

"Everyone here can speak English. Why should I learn Welsh?"

"It's fun to be able to speak more than one language. I speak French and German; they're easier to learn than Welsh, but some of the Welsh words are like the French words. 'Eglws' means a church in Welsh and 'eglise' means a church in French. 'Fenetre' is the French for window; 'Fenestr' is the Welsh. 'Ci' is a dog. 'Ci drwg' means bad dog and 'Ci da' means good dog."

"Ci drwg," Martin said, without thinking, and then looked at Blue. His ears had gone flat. There was a miserable expression in his eyes. His tail drooped.

"Someone used to say that to him. Look at him," Tom said. "Can't have that. He hasn't deserved a scolding."

He laughed and patted his leg.

"Come on, then. Good dog, Blue. Ci da. Clever fellow." His voice was joyous and the dog brightened, his ears flicking up and his tail waving. He licked Tom's hand.

"It takes so little to upset him. We'll have to be careful. He's a dog that can't take scolding. People think these German Shepherds are tough, but a lot of them are extremely sensitive and if you raise your voice to them, get very bothered indeed."

Tom looked at Martin and grinned. The whole family laughed so much; his own family were much more serious. And they weren't his family, he reminded himself. None of them understood him. He couldn't stand up to scolding either. His insides knotted and he felt sick when people were angry with him. And they were, so often.

Tom was still talking.

"Dogs can hear a beetle walk across the grass and an engine at a distance of almost a mile away, maybe more. Our noisy voices must shatter their ear drums."

He smiled at Martin.

"Don't look so worried. Think of all the fun you can have with Blue when he's trained. They're marvellous dogs to own."

"I was afraid of dogs till Blue came. But he was so miserable; nobody could be afraid of him."

"Dogs are OK," Tom said. "People often aren't. They expect animals to be cuddly and sweet and they aren't. Dogs don't like being patted on the head by strangers any more than you or I do. It may startle them; it frightens some. They have to learn about people, and often people expect them to know without being taught. You have to know a dog well before you can take liberties."

He stroked Blue gently again.

"We wouldn't like people to come up and slap us on the back when we didn't know them. Why should a dog be treated as if he had no feelings or fears?"

He put his arm round Martin and squeezed his shoulder. "Tag wants a game of football. I haven't time today, as I have to write an article and have it in the post first thing on Monday. Will you play with him? Tie Blue to the towbar. He'll be happy enough so long as you don't go out of sight."

Tag erupted from the caravan in a blaze of excitement.

"Come on," he yelled. "I'm going to be a footballer and play in the World Cup. I'm going to be the bestest footballer ever."

"You'll never do any good if you screech like that," his mother said, on her way to the Land Rover. "Coke and cookies for you too, Martin, in the trailer, at eleven."

"Cookies? Trailer? " Martin was baffled.

Meg Pritchard laughed.

"Oh gee, I always forget. You call them biscuits and the trailer is what you call a caravan."

"And that's a trashcan," said Tag, pointing to the dustbin. "And Mom carries a pocket book, not a handbag, and walks on the sidewalk, not the pavement."

"Don't worry about it, Martin," Meg said. "The children won't confuse you. Tom and I probably will. We'd lived all our lives in America before we moved here. But the children have spent a large part of their lives in Wales. They're practically natives."

"Cymru am bydd," Tag said. Martin did know that that meant "Wales for ever". Maybe if Tag could learn to speak Welsh, he could too. He wasn't going to be beaten by a six year old. He determined to put aside a couple of hours a day, and to listen to the family, and try to understand them when they spoke Welsh.

Martin would show them all he wasn't as stupid as they thought. But he didn't want anyone in the family to know he was learning their language. He would have to find someone who could help him, someone who could be relied on not to tell them. One day he'd astound them all by joining in their conversation as if he had been born a Welshman.

Tag was filled with excitement that spilled over into unruliness. He played by his own rules, kicking the ball hard in the wrong direction, throwing it so that it hit Martin in the face, bouncing it against the caravan wall until his father shouted at him to stop.

Tag didn't know how to stop. Excitement had mastered him, and he was beyond sense.

He kicked hard again. The ball rolled past Blue. The dog, who was lying quietly, stood up as Tag ran by. Tag reached out, grabbed Blue's tail and tweaked it hard. Blue squealed with pain and bolted under the caravan, as far as the line would take him.

Martin, infuriated, ran after Tag, turned him round, tugged his hair hard and shouted at him.

"Don't you dare ever do that to any dog again."

Tag kicked Martin's leg, and began to howl. His father erupted from the caravan.

"How can anyone work in this madhouse?" Tom was angry. "What's the matter with Tag?"

"He pulled Blue's tail. I pulled his hair," Martin said, sure he would now be banned from visiting again, ever. "I'm sorry. He hurt Blue and made me mad. I wanted him to know how Blue felt."

"I'm very inclined to pull his hair myself," Tom said. "Tag, inside and no argument. Wash your face and get our drinks and cookies ready. I don't want you out here again until I say you may come."

Tag glared at his father, put out his tongue at Martin, and stamped up the steps into the caravan."

"One thing," Tom Pritchard said, down on his knees, peering under the caravan. "That dog of yours is sweet tempered; or he would have bitten Tag. Which would have served the little monkey right. He won't learn sense."

"Blue hates being hurt. He's a big softie." Like me, Martin thought and was surprised at the idea. Maybe he and his dog both had to learn to be tougher.

It took over ten minutes to convince Blue that nobody intended to hurt him. He followed Martin up the steps and into the van. Tag was sitting at the table, a book in front of him, but he wasn't reading. He stood up, and at once Blue sat, his tail firmly tucked underneath him, leaning against Tom's leg, asking for protection.

As Tag approached him, he moved behind Martin.

"Now you've made him afraid of you," Tom said. "It will be a long time before he learns to trust you. Which means you can't come and watch when Martin has his lessons. Blue won't work at all if you are there. He'll always be thinking you're going to pull his tail again."

Tag's voice, when he spoke, was forlorn.

"How can I make him unafraid?"

"It won't be easy," Tom said. "I don't even know if you can. Blue's sized you up as a child that dogs must avoid. He's been hurt by people in the past; and you've undone some of the work Martin's put in."

"I didn't think," Tag said.

"You never do."

Tag looked at his father, then walked out of the room, slamming the door behind him. Martin knew just how he felt. He wished life wasn't so difficult.

He drank his coke and ate the fudge cookies, leashed Blue, and began the walk back. But he didn't want to go home. There would be nothing much to do when he reached the farm. The sun was bright, though there was frost in the air, and winter seemed to prevent spring from coming.

He decided to take the long way back.

The path led past the Lump. He stared at the great rock thrusting itself into the sky, dwarfing the little cottage that crouched beneath it. Water poured from a rocky shelf high above the road and cascaded into a stream that bordered the road.

As they passed the cottage garden Blue pricked his ears, and pulled on his lead.

"No," Martin said, as the dog tried to drag him through the half open gate.

Blue barked.

"What on earth?" Blue never barked when they were walking.

Then he heard a voice calling. A small voice, an old voice, that quavered and shook.

"Help, please help."

Martin raced through the gate, Blue pulling desperately, as if he knew that something was very wrong indeed.

Chapter 13

The tiny front garden was winter weary, and unkempt with last year's dead flowerheads. But daffodils bloomed in clumps and crocuses starred the grass.

Blue was pulling hard now, and Martin followed him. Through the creaking wicket gate, up the crazy paving path, round the back of the cottage, and into a terraced garden that followed the outline of the hill.

Steps twisted between heather banks that were smothered with gold and dark green foliage and flowers of purple, pink, and white. Daffodils grew between the clumps, and flowering bushes, starred with white flowers, gleamed above them.

Martin stared at what seemed to be a bundle of clothing lying at the foot of the steps. A thin hand waved to him.

The old lady lay in a crumpled heap, her leg twisted under her. She spoke in Welsh, and Martin, for the first time, wished that he understood the language.

"I'm sorry. I don't speak Welsh," he said. It suddenly seemed a ridiculous failing.

"I fell. I think I've broken my leg . . . so silly," she said. Her voice was a gasping breath, almost inaudible. "The kitchen door . . . open. Phone, boy. Get help. Leave . . . dog . . . here. Company. Like . . . dogs. Can't have one now . . . " Her voice tailed away.

The long line was in his pocket. Martin tied Blue to the thin trunk of a little tree that stood beside the old lady. She reached out to pat the dog, and he lay down, his nose on her hand, as if he knew she needed comfort.

Martin had never felt so helpless in his life. He didn't know any first aid, but he did know that she shouldn't be allowed to lie there in the cold.

The cottage was tiny inside, but bright with colour. Honeysuckle twined over the floral wallpaper. Cushions embroidered with brilliant fluttering butterflies were flung casually on the chairs and there were several more scattered over a long settee. Photographs of children covered every wall.

No one seemed to know anything about Megan the Lump. The children at school said she was a witch. No witch could live in a house as happy as

130

this. A blue budgerigar chirped a welcome from a cage in the window.

A bright fire blazed cheerfully, reflected in the willow pattern plates on the Welsh dresser. It was very cold outside. Martin ran into the little bedroom that led out of the sitting room. He pulled the eiderdown and a blanket off the bed and raced into the garden.

"You need to be warm," he said. He wondered if he could get the blanket beneath the old lady, but though thin, she was heavy and he was afraid he would hurt her leg even more. He covered her, seeing pain in her dark eyes and the set of her mouth.

She gripped his hand.

"Sensible boy. Phone," she said.

Martin ran in again. Who did he phone? He dialled 999, intending to call an ambulance, but put the phone down before it started to ring. He had no idea of Megan's correct address. He didn't even know her surname. The hospital was in Bangor; the Ysbyty Gwynedd; or would it be the one in Holyhead? He didn't know that either. The cottage was out in the wilds, even more remote from the main road than Bryn Gwynt. It wasn't much use telling someone from twenty miles away that the ambulance had to come to Megan the Lump. The cottage wasn't anywhere near a major road, but on a very narrow back lane. He didn't know which village it was in either.

131

There was no house name on the door or the gate.

He raced back to ask the old lady. He looked at her in horror. Her eyes were closed, her face grey. She didn't answer when he spoke. He ran in again, feeling sick.

He dialled his home number.

He listened to the endless ring. "Mum, be there, please God, let her be there." Would no one ever answer?

"Mum?" He had never been so pleased to hear her voice. The words spilled out so fast that Leah had to ask him to slow down.

"I'm at Megan the Lump. She's fallen and broken her leg; I don't know the name of her home and she's unconscious. I can't tell the ambulance where to come."

"Stay with her and try and keep her warm. I'll find Gwyn; I don't know either, but I'll organize it. Don't leave her alone, whatever you do, Martin. Can you manage?"

"I can't do much," Martin said, as his mother rang off. He went back to sit on the bottom step and watch the old lady. There was nothing he could do. He bent down to see if she were still breathing, and relaxed as he heard the faint sound she was making.

"Please, God, don't let her die," he said, talking to the air, to himself, and to Blue. He untied the dog and Blue lay down beside him. If only someone would come. If only he had a

132

watch. The minutes passed endlessly. How long before the ambulance came?

The cottage was surrounded by deserted fields. In the distance sheep and cattle moved. The mountains on the mainland were black against the sky, their soaring tops hidden in grey cloud. He knew that old Megan lived alone, that the children mocked and teased her, that she bought her milk from Jones the Milk.

Blue pricked his ears.

Moments later the ambulance braked outside the gate. Martin tied Blue up again, and ran round the cottage to the front garden.

The two men moved swiftly, taking a stretcher and blankets from the vehicle. The older man spoke to Martin in Welsh, as the boy led the way into the back garden.

"I don't speak Welsh," he said, for the second time that day. Everyone seemed sure that he did. He would have to learn. He was being stupid. He understood that now. People spoke their own language in their own country.

"Who are you?" one of the men asked. "Are you her son?"

"Martin Slater, from the farm down the road. My dog heard her calling for help, and he brought me in here."

"Good job he did. She owes him her life. She could have lain here for days without anyone finding her, out in the wilds like this."

Megan was lifted gently and wrapped in the

blankets.

"We'll be off. Someone will need to see her cottage is locked up safely. Find her relatives, and things like that."

Which was all very well, Martin thought, but where did he start?

He watched the ambulance drive away. He stared at the cottage, wondering what he ought to do.

He left Blue tied to the tree and went inside. The old lady's handbag was on the kitchen table. Would there be keys in it? If he locked the place up and she didn't have a key, could she get in again? Did she keep a key hidden somewhere outside, as they did at the farm? He looked in the obvious places, but there was no key under any flowerpot, under any ledge, or under the dustbin. No key hung in the little shed, which was bare except for a heap of folded sacks, and a box containing apples neatly wrapped in newspaper.

A Land Rover drew up at the gate. Gwyn jumped out.

"They've taken her to the hospital," Martin said. "They told me to lock up. Only she hasn't got her bag or keys with her; she hasn't anything with her."

"Difficult, boy," Gwyn said. "I don't know who her friends are, or if she has any. She's a strange old lady and people tend to avoid her." He opened a cupboard door.

"We'll have to look after the budgie. Can't leave it here alone, poor bird." He looked around him. "I'll check that all the windows are shut. Then we'll take her bag with us. I'll have to make sure her keys are in it. Don't like this, boy. Feel like a burglar. Has to be done, though."

He was looking around him as he spoke. There was a fire guard in a corner of the room. He set it in front of the grate.

"Your mother's going to ring the hospital later to see how the old lady is and if there's anything we can do. She may want her own nightclothes, and toilet things."

Martin watched as Gwyn shut the kitchen window and locked and bolted the back door.

"Keys on a ring in her bag. Better just check they fit the front door. We don't want her to have to break her way in when she comes home."

"She'll be away a long time," Martin said. "She can't look after herself with a broken leg."

Gwyn frowned as he looked around the room. "You don't think of the difficulties people have when they live alone. There's food for the budgie in the cupboard. We can take that till your mother goes into town. At least we know what he needs."

He lifted the cage, picked up the shabby brown handbag, and handed them to Martin.

"I'd better just check the food she's left. Might go off and smell nasty when she comes back. Bread and milk and things like that. Put her bag

135

and the cage in the Land Rover, boy. Coming back with me, or walking Blue?"

"I'll walk Blue," Martin said. "It won't take long across the field path."

He was aware, on his way down the hill, of a lifting of his mood. His stepfather had treated him like another adult, trusting him, discussing problems with him. All the same, he was worried about the old lady, concerned for her, feeling that if she died it would somehow be his fault, because he hadn't been able to do enough to help her when she needed help so badly. It might be an idea to take a course in first aid. Tag had needed help too.

He had a sudden vision of himself, competent, clever, able to do more than other people when disaster struck. If he learned First Aid and also how to climb, he and Blue could join the Mountain Rescue team. They'd be able to ride in helicopters and be winched down on to the mountains. A Mountain Rescue climber had come to give a talk at his school, and brought his dog.

He had shown the class the jacket the dog wore, with the heavy harness and shackle that anchored him in the helicopter, and the light that clipped onto the jacket, so that he could be seen while hunting on the mountains for victims of climbing or walking accidents.

"People always have accidents when its bitter cold or blowing a gale or snowing," the man had said. "Or there's wicked ice that freezes on your eyes and mouth and nose, and on the dog's fur, and makes the going lethal."

Now, when the helicopter went over at night, when Martin was safe in bed, he thought of the men on the hills, of the siren that made them scramble and race across the tarmac, clambering in while the great blades scythed the sky.

Then up into the darkness, heading for the towering cliffs, courting danger over and over again. The little swift animals would quarter the hillside, and another human would owe his or her life to a dog.

Martin hadn't had Blue then, and hadn't thought much about dog training.

Blue had probably saved the old lady's life. Maybe they could save more lives.

He was home before he realized it. Blue walked sedately beside him, as if aware that he had played an important role and must now behave like a sensible dog.

They ran down the last part of the path and into the farm kitchen.

His mother was making sandwiches.

"Did you phone? Is she going to be all right?" he asked, almost out of breath.

"Yes. It'll take time. She's not in danger, though she might well have died if you and Blue hadn't happened along. You were very sensible, Martin. I'm proud of you." Leah was buttering bread, working fast as she was late with lunch.

She sliced a cooked tongue and gave Martin the horseradish cream.

"Put that on each piece, and then add a slice of lettuce," she said, taking it for granted that Martin would help. She worked swiftly, with so many people to feed.

Martin felt as if he had just been rewarded with the Victoria Cross. It was ages since his mother had praised him for anything.

" Poor Megan's suffering from shock and some degree of hypothermia," Leah added another sandwich to the growing pile. "But they say her heart's strong and she's very healthy for her age. It's a simple break, and she ought to get over it well."

"You did a good job, boy", Taid said, shedding his wellingtons on the doormat and walking in his socks across to the sink to wash his hands. Martin, suddenly ravenously hungry, took a sandwich. He suddenly remembered an absurd phrase of Tag's. He felt gruntled, instead of disgruntled. He grinned to himself.

Blue retreated to his usual place behind the big armchair in the corner, in which Anna Wyn sat, her face intent. She held something in her hand.

"Come and see," she said.

She was dripping milk, from a small eye dropper, into one of the smallest creatures Martin had ever seen. It was about an inch long, black, and at first he thought it was an outsize beetle.

He looked at it with total disbelief. It was so

tiny. It was also the strangest shape. He bent and saw the oddest little face.

"It's a baby bat," he said. "How on earth did you get it?"

"It's mother flew into someone's kitchen. She was so terrified that she dropped it on the table. They cling to the mother's fur."

Martin was fascinated. He watched the little animal swallow, each drop looking bigger than its mouth. "What will you do with it?" he asked.

"If we can keep it alive it'll be fun to have in the sanctuary. We won't be able to let it go, ever." Anna Wyn put down the syringe and shifted the baby bat on to her other hand. "I rang a vet who specializes in bats. She says that they don't know how to look after themselves or feed themselves when they've been hand reared. We can't teach them how to fly after insects. It apparently doesn't just come naturally."

"All young things have to be taught," Taid said.

As Martin watched, the baby shifted on Anna Wyn's hand, and suddenly scratched its side with the smallest leg Martin had ever seen.

"Aren't you afraid of breaking it?" he asked.

"I'm more afraid of killing it with the wrong kind of food. Or too much; or too little. It's impossible to know how much it ought to have; and nobody makes bat's milk. Can't just catch one and milk it either," Anna Wyn said, and Martin wasn't sure whether she were joking or not. He never was sure, with Anna Wyn.

Then he realized that Anna Wyn had said "bat" the day before, not bats. She was talking about the creature in the box she was carrying. She hadn't been making fun of him at all. She had been excited by her new patient and wanting to share the news.

Martin reached out a finger and stroked the velvet soft back. The thick fine hair was so short and dense that it was impossible to see the separate strands. It was hard to believe this was an animal related to dogs rather than to birds. The wings were so fragile that they seemed as if they could never grow to adult size and fly.

Anna Wyn put it into its bed, lying it on a wad of paper tissues. It clung there, not moving. She covered the box with a lid of gauze, held on by a rubber band, and put it close to the Aga.

"I wonder if it misses its mother," Martin said.

"Sure to, poor little object." Anna Wyn put a rubber band round the gauze, to keep it in place. "I hope it survives. We seem to be getting the oddest creatures in now we've advertised the sanctuary."

"Mouths to feed," Taid said. "A lot of money to satisfy them. Fish for the sea birds and mealworms for the land birds, and those don't come cheap."

"Nothing comes cheap," Gwyn came in through the door, shedding his boots. He washed his hands at the sink, and took a sandwich. "Anna Wyn, there's a newcomer for you in the Land

Rover, and old Megan's handbag is there too. I had to take the feed out, and forgot to bring them in."

Anna Wyn went outside and returned carrying the budgie in his cage. She set it on the table by the window, moving an azalea plant that Leah was cherishing.

"We'll need a high hook for him," Taid said. "Or the cats will scare the life out of him."

"We can put him outside with the animals in the childrens' park," Leah said. "He'll be an added attraction; if he is a he," she added.

"When do you open?" Martin was suddenly curious.

"On Monday. We've put handbills in the shops in Menai bridge, and in the bank and in some of the garages. Also in the Little Chefs."

"Blue will have to be penned when you aren't around," Gwyn said. "People are afraid of German Shepherds. He'll have to learn to accept the visitors, and not bark at them."

"Have to watch the gates," Leah said, passing the sandwich plate to Taid, who was looking worried. "Otherwise we'll have animals all over the place."

"Just going to say that myself," he said. "All kinds of people there'll be, and children. Need to teach them how to behave with animals and how to behave in the country too. Some of them never have seen a sheep or a goat before."

"Cariad will teach them their manners," said

Anna Wyn. "She'll stand no nonsense. She's a very useful creature."

Martin, remembering his own battles with the old ewe thought some children might be in for a considerable shock. A moment later he realized that he had begun to think in quite a different way since he had found Blue.

He turned his head as a tall boy came into the kitchen, and greeted everyone with a grin. His dark hair was neatly cut to just below his ears and brown eyes flashed happily at everyone.

"Mike," Anna Wyn said. "It's been a long time."

"I heard about the sanctuary. I've nothing to do over Easter and I'm already bored with the holidays. Could you do with some help?"

"We could do with all of you," Anna Wyn said.

"Jennet might come. Laura won't. You know how she feels about animals."

"They all either kick or bite, or butt," Gwyn said, laughing. "Or stink. Your sister is very fussy."

"She's a pain," Mike said. Martin had placed him now. Mike Granit, who lived in the cottage at the end of Little Lane, that led to the church. "All Laura ever wants to do is paint," her brother added.

"Suggest she paints animals," Anna Wyn said. "Then we can put the pictures up in local shops and get some free publicity."

"It would make a change from mountains," Mike looked at Martin. "I know you from school, don't I?"

Martin nodded. Mike must be at least three years older than he, and in a much higher form, but he had seen him around.

"You saved young Tag the day he was trying to pick a fossil rock out of the wall for me," Mike said. "Come to think of it, Tag and Midge might help too."

"Midge would be useful," Anna Wyn said. "Tag's a disaster all by himself, no matter what he does."

Mike took a sandwich from the plate that Leah handed him, and bit into it.

"Mmmmm. This is good. You must come and tell my mum how to make my lunch box," he said. "I might get a change from sardines. She doesn't know anything else exists!" He laughed as he spoke, and Martin was pretty sure that that statement wasn't true.

Martin was just about to take another sandwich himself when Blue raced to the window and began to bark, long and loud and excitedly.

"Trouble," Gwyn said, looking out of the window.

Everybody ran outside, Blue ahead of them, behaving in a way that nobody had seen before.

Chapter 14

There was pandemonium outside. Blue was barking, someone was shouting, the pigs were squealing, and both farm dogs were adding their voices to the din.

Gradually Martin realized that there were two voices, both yelling frantically.

"Get your dog off."

Blue had two boys penned inside the chicken run, in which they had taken shelter, while he barked at them from outside. It was some minutes before Martin could quiet his dog, and until then nobody could make themselves heard.

"Our first visitors," Anna Wyn said, "and your beastly dog has to scare them off."

"I doubt if they're here for any good purpose," Mike Granit frowned. "I know them too well.

Come on out, both of you. The dog wasn't going to hurt you. He was doing his job."

They came out, their faces sullen. Martin recognized them and felt sick. His two tormentors had tracked him down and he was no longer safe at home. Even with his family there, he felt the familiar closing of his throat, the shudder that couldn't be controlled, the panic that threatened to overwhelm him, and that always prevented him from running.

Blue was still growling. Martin could feel the throb through the dog's collar.

"What do you want?" Gwyn asked. "I know you both, don't I? Mervyn Hughes, and Dai Evans. We don't open till Monday. It said so, very plainly, in the advertisements."

"Wanted to see what you'd got. We're friends of Martin. He asked us," the older boy said, convinced that Martin would be too afraid of retribution later to deny it.

Gwyn looked at Martin.

"Did you invite them?"

Martin took a deep breath. He had to stand up to them now, or he never would. He shook his head.

"No one invites them," Mike said. "Wherever they go, there's trouble. Trouble at school. Trouble in the village. They rip up plants, break branches off trees, paint slogans on walls and cars; vandal's their middle name." He looked at them with intense dislike.

145

All very well for him, Martin thought. He's nearly a head taller than either of them and much bigger in every way.

Mike looked at them, brooding. "The thing is, what have they been up to? Or did Blue prevent something happening?"

"We've not done anything," the bigger boy said. Martin was not yet sure which was which. The speaker was a burly boy, with dark haird framing a scowling face. He relied on his excessive weight to help him manipulate any situation. But his weight hindered him. If he were alone Martin could easily outrun him. But the other boy was fast, very fast, and it never paid to run away. It was worse when caught.

Martin was much more afraid of the younger of the two, who twisted arms, thumped ribs, and kicked shins, while his companion urged him on, laughing.

Gwyn glanced around the yard. The door of the feed store shed was open. He walked over and looked inside. Two large bags of feed had been slashed from top to bottom. Their contents spilled all over the floor, mixed in with something white from another bag at the far end of the shed.

"That's forty pounds your dads owe me," Gwyn said. "That's lime you've mixed with the feed. The whole lot's unusable."

"We didn't do it. We found it like that. Young Martin here did it. Everyone knows he hates living here."

"Everyone's wrong," Gwyn said. "That's his dog food you spoiled, that he paid for himself. Not going to ruin that, is he? He's been out all morning, most of the time with me. Police job, isn't it? Trespass . . . wilful damage. And what else did you intend?"

"They damaged the children's playground last week," Mike said. "My dad's had trouble with them too. Though people rarely catch them at it, they always know who's responsible."

"We can sue you," the bigger boy said. "Your dog attacked us. Dangerous dog that, it ought to be put down. And your sheep kicked me."

Cariad was standing at the far side of the yard. She was behaving as if she might have been kicked in return. Martin felt a sudden twinge of sympathy for her, as she stood, head down, looking utterly miserable.

"You had no business on the property." Gwyn was angry.

Mike bent down and sniffed the spilled feed.

"Your feed's not only mixed with lime; it's been soaked in paraffin," he said. "Smell it. I wonder if they intended to set light to it afterwards?"

Gwyn stared, and bent down in his turn. He stood up, a furious expression on his face.

"I'm not sending for the police," he said. "I'm taking the law into my own hands."

"You can't. What are you going to do?"

"Your fathers will do it for me. Mervyn, your father supplied that feed. He'll replace the spoiled

147

feed; and if there's any more trouble from you in any way at all, I'll change my supplier." Gwyn's voice shook with anger. "I spend a great deal of money with your father each year, and so do my friends. Money that helps buy food and clothes for you and your family. The village will support me; it's up to you."

"Please don't tell Da." It was the younger boy speaking. So that was Mervyn. He looked as if he was terrified of his father finding out what he had done. Serve him right, Martin thought. He would have to find money for another sack of dog food and that one had cost nearly thirty pounds, which he had earned by working on odd jobs round the farm during the last few weeks.

Cheaper to buy in bulk, Gywn said. It would have been; but now he wished it had been a three kilo bag instead of fifteen kilos.

"Your father needs to know. Or you'll end up in bad trouble. The police aren't stupid. It's easier to find out wrong doers in a village than a town." The bigger boy fidgeted uneasily as Gwyn faced him. " As for you, young Dai, your father's my contract shearer. I've four hundred sheep here he won't be seeing at all if I've any more trouble from you."

Gwyn glanced at Martin's face, and guessed the situation. "Or if you take it out on Martin. There's plenty more that would like the work. I'll be ringing your fathers this evening. Count them as friends and doing them a good turn, keeping you out of jail. I'd be sorry to take away my business. But just remember, it isn't a threat, it's a promise. Now get out."

Martin watched them go.

"You do know them, don't you?" Gwyn asked when they were out of sight. "They're both older than you."

"Martin knows them," Mike said. He had been watching the younger boy. "They're both bullies, but it's hard to catch them as the boys they bully are too afraid to tell. They've been having a go at you, haven't they?"

Martin nodded.

"Lost school books; bad reports because your books are scribbled in . . . was that due to those two?" Gwyn asked.

"Yes," Martin said. "It's no use telling anyone; they lie in wait and catch you when you're on your own. They take your pocket money too. It isn't only me; a lot of the little boys are terrified of them."

"I don't think they'll be round here in a hurry," Gwyn said. "Any more trouble, Martin, you tell me. Understood? If we let them get away with it, they'll get worse. I'll have a word with your headmaster. If they're stopped now, they might just grow up human."

Martin, remembering some of the unhappier sessions with the two, had his doubts.

"You come up to our house and walk with me to the school bus," Mike said. "It's only about half a mile in the wrong direction. I'll come in on the bus instead of cycling. I'm bigger than they are and they know I won't stand for any nonsense."

Anna Wyn had been checking her animals.

"I was afraid they might have hurt some of them," she said.

"Can I look round?" Martin asked. He had never been interested enough before, but something was changing him. Gwyn had taken his side, had dealt with one of his major fears, and he had also found a new friend. Mike would be much more fun than Tag. Tag was fine, but he was only six years old, and there was so much a little boy would fail to understand.

"We're almost ready," Anna Wyn said. "Not quite. Still a few odd jobs to do." She led the way through a wicket gate into the field next to the house. This was now mown and laid out with flower beds, which Taid intended to plant with bedding plants in the summer.

He had been very busy indeed. There were five large cages, filled with birds. Cockatiels and finches, two magpies and a raven, a pheasant recovering from a broken wing, a barn owl that winked at Martin with its one good eye. No one knew how it had been blinded in the other. It also had only half a wing.

"Ollie's a pet," Anna Wyn said. "He likes people and being looked at and will perch for hours on my shoulder."

Beyond the aviaries was a large mound, enclosed by a low brick wall. On top of it was a hutch, and here Anna Wyn had a number of guinea pigs of all colours, busy running around, chasing one another, or feeding.

Six geese wandered round the field, following anyone they thought might have titbits. They were much smaller than English geese, with brown markings and a soft forlorn cry.

"They were given to us," Anna Wynn said. "Nobody seems to know what breed they are. Have to find out sometime. We want to put labels on the cages."

Harriet, the pot bellied pig, had her own run. Most of her family had been sold, but three little pigs remained and came up to the fence, snorting and grunting. Harriet nosed them out of the way, and carried on her own conversation with Mike who laughed at her and answered her back.

"This is Dolly, and her foal," Anna Wyn said, as a little Shetland pranced towards her, the tiny baby by her side. Mike moved towards them and the foal skidded to a halt, shied, and ran behind its mother, out of the way of patting hands. There was a small barn beside the wicket gate. Martin realized that everyone must have been working flat out.

The part of the barn nearest to the gate was laid out as a small shop. There were books to buy and toy animals; postcards pictured birds, and one shelf was filled with models of British wild animals. Beyond it were small tables and chairs, where visitors could eat the snacks Martin's mother planned to produce.

"I can help here, at weekends and in the holidays," Mike said. "It would be fun. I've always wanted to be involved in something like this. Laura could paint pictures to put up and brighten the walls."

"I've all kinds of plans," Anna Wyn said. "I want one of those miniature horses; and glass tanks for fish; and a pool for the ducks and geese. And a paddling pool for the children on hot days."

Martin's mother put her head over the gate.

"Martin, Megan Pritchard's asking for you. I said we'd drive over and see her. She's worrying about the cottage and her bird."

Martin had a great deal to think of as they drove to the mainland. He had never been in a hospital and found it daunting. He stopped at the flower stands.

"Can we buy her some flowers?"

"Yes, and a magazine too," Leah said, and went to choose a couple for her, while Martin bought a bunch of daffodils.

The old lady was propped up against the pillows in a ward which seemed to Martin to be full of people.

"Want to thank you, Bach," she said, and for once Martin didn't resent someone not using his proper name. Bach, he thought, meant small one, or young one. He wasn't very sure. There was a sheepdog called Bach on the next farm.

"My father locked up. We've got your budgie till you come home," Martin said.

"I can go in and make fires and keep the place warm and dusted." Leah smiled. "A house gets so damp and unwelcoming if its empty for long."

"I've no one," the old lady said. "Just me and the little bird. I owe you, Bach."

Martin looked at her and thought, while his mother took the daffodils, hoping to find a nurse and ask for a vase. The old lady must be lonely, living there all by herself without neighbours. She rarely went out, and most of the village seemed to regard her with distrust. She was a misfit, like himself.

"I'm glad I came by," he said. "But it was my dog who found you, not me."

Megan looked at him.

"We're loners, you and me. I don't know how to thank you, Bach, but there's one thing I can do, when I come home."

"What's that?" Martin asked.

"I was a teacher once, long ago. Don't speak Welsh, do you?"

Martin shook his head.

"You want to learn?"

"Yes," he said, and meant it.

Megan sighed.

"Life's not easy, boy," she said. "Everything changes all the time and some of us never quite belong. You're one of those; so am I. I was a stepchild too. My father was a cruel man and hated me. Beat me and I had never had enough food to eat. Your life's ahead. Your new Da's a good man."

She leaned back on her pillows, and closed hr eyes wearily. She opened them, with an effort, and smiled at Martin.

"Everything to look forward to, Bach," she said, opening her eyes again. "You need courage; and kindness. And you've got both. You'll do."

Martin, looking out at the mountains as they left the hospital car park, thought that it had been a very odd day. A great deal had happened.

That evening he walked with Blue on the hill, and looked down on the farm and knew that at least he had nothing to fear from the bullies any more. School would improve. He would learn to speak Welsh and even though he didn't belong to this family, he had been accepted. Everything was going to change.

He was in the big field, which was escape proof. He took off Blue's lead, and whistled to the dog and the pair of them raced through the grass, the dog jumping up at him as he ran.

Down below them the farm lay in the evening sunlight, and the lambs skipped in the next field, chasing one another, until all were lost and began to baa in forlorn voices. The deep bleats of the ewes answered them. Martin watched in amusement as each lamb found its own mother.

He had never really looked at the sheep before or noticed what they were doing.

A moment later there was sudden panic, and all the flock began to run. Martin looked across the field. A dog was chasing the sheep; a strange dog that he had never seen before.

He vaulted the gate and ran, waving his arms and shouting. he picked up a stone and hurled it, and the dog, seeing him, turned and fled, down the field and through a gap in the hedge. Martin followed and pulled sticks across to mark the gap. If they weren't careful the lambs would escape through there.

Gwyn raced towards him. His eyes raked the sheepfield.

"He didn't have time to hurt any of them. Good work, son," he said. "Now let's block that gap before we get any more trouble."

Martin, helping carry the fencing across the field, thought back to a year ago. He had been terrified of dogs. Now he hadn't thought twice.

Blue, left alone in the empty field, barked mournfully.

"We might train him for sheep," Gwyn said. "He's coming on well."

They blocked the gap and walked companionably together across the field, collecting Blue as they went. That evening Martin joined in making plans for the sanctuary. He felt as if he had come a very long way in the last twenty four hours, and the future was no longer to be feared.

There was a place in it for both him and for Blue.

It was the first time he had ever felt excited at the thought of the years ahead.